Praise for John Banville

"If Banville is capable of writing an unmemorable sentence, he has successfully concealed the evidence." —*The Washington Post*

"Banville is a master at capturing the most fleeting memory or excruciating twinge of self-awareness with riveting accuracy." —*People*

"Prodigiously gifted. He cannot write an unpolished phrase, so we read him slowly, relishing the stream of pleasures he affords. Everything in Banville's books is alive. Bleakly elegant, he is a writer's writer . . . who can conjure with the poetry of people and places." —*The Independent* (London)

"Banville is the heir to Proust, via Nabokov."
—*The Daily Beast*

"A glorious stylist whose prose holds sustaining pleasures, both large and small."

"Banville's mastery of languag[illegible]
delight." —*Evening S*[illegible]

D1167194

ALSO BY JOHN BANVILLE

Nightspawn

Birchwood

Doctor Copernicus

Kepler

The Newton Letter

Mefisto

The Book of Evidence

Ghosts

Athena

The Untouchable

Eclipse

Shroud

The Sea

The Infinities

Ancient Light

John Banville

LONG LANKIN

John Banville, the author of sixteen novels, has been the recipient of the Man Booker Prize, the James Tait Black Memorial Prize, the Guardian Fiction Award, the Franz Kafka Prize, and a Lannan Literary Award for Fiction. He lives in Dublin.

INTERNATIONAL

LONG LANKIN

STORIES

John Banville

VINTAGE INTERNATIONAL
Vintage Books
A Division of Random House, Inc.
New York

FIRST VINTAGE INTERNATIONAL EDITION, JULY 2013

Copyright © 1970, 1984 by John Banville

All rights reserved. Published in the United States by Vintage Books, a division of Random House, Inc., New York and in Canada by Random House of Canada Limited, Toronto. Originally published in different form in Great Britain by Secker and Warburg, London, in 1970, and subsequently published in Ireland by The Gallery Press, Meath, in 1984.

Vintage is a registered trademark and Vintage International and colophon are trademarks of Random House, Inc.

This is a work of fiction. Names, characters, places, events, and incidents either are the product of the author's imagination or are used fictitiously. Any resemblance to actual persons, living or dead, events, or locales is entirely coincidental.

The Cataloging-in-Publication Data is on file at the Library of Congress.

Vintage ISBN: 978-0-345-80706-9

Book design by Claudia Martinez

www.vintagebooks.com

Printed in the United States of America
10 9 8 7 6 5 4 3 2 1

My lady came down she was thinking no harm

Long Lankin stood ready to catch her in his arm

CENTRAL ARKANSAS LIBRARY SYSTEM
LITTLE ROCK PUBLIC LIBRARY
100 ROCK STREET
LITTLE ROCK, ARKANSAS 72201

CONTENTS

LONG LANKIN

WILD WOOD

A fine rain began to fall, it drifted soundlessly through the tangled branches and settled on the carpet of dead leaves on the ground. The boy turned up the collar of his jacket and crouched by the fire. He was cold. About him the wood was silent, yet beneath the silence there were movements and strange sounds, strange stirrings and rustlings in the trees. He shivered, and blew into his cupped hands. A burning branch fell in a shower of sparks from the fire and rolled near his feet, hissing in the wet leaves. In the hazel grove behind him a tuneless whistle rose, punctuated by the dull cracks of an axe wounding wood. He stood up and went into the trees.

—Is the fire all right? Horse asked, turning with the axe held above his shoulder.

—Yes, said the boy.

—You didn't put any of them green branches on it?

—I only used the dry wood like you said.

He made another chop at the branch before him and muttered:

—They'd see the smoke.

Horse was sixteen, a great hulking boy whose clothes never fitted because he outgrew them while they were still new. He had a raw bony face and huge hands, and a mop of carroty red hair sprouted up from his skull like the stalks of a root vegetable. Horse knew the wood from which the best bows could be made, and he had a secret method of hammering nails flat for arrowheads. He could build a fire in the worst conditions, and he knew how to skin and cook a rabbit. Such gifts made him the natural leader of the gang, but he never acknowledged this leadership, and seemed unaware of the unspoken honour. A strange wild creature who rarely spoke and never smiled, his own secret lonely ways took all his concentration.

The boy sat down on the rotten stump of a tree and looked at his hands.

—Horse, he said. Are you going to school tomorrow?

Horse said nothing, but went on chopping at the branch as if he had not heard. The boy went on:

—I think I better go in tomorrow. If I mitch again they might send someone home to my aunt to see what's wrong. Then they'd find out and I'd be in trouble.

—Here, said Horse. Peel that.

He threw the long branch like a spear and it plunged into the ground at the boy's feet, then he turned back and attacked another part of the tree. The boy pulled the branch from the ground and with his penknife began to peel away the bark in long green strips.

—Well you won't be going in tomorrow then, Horse?

For a while there was no reply, then Horse said violently:

—Not going back anymore. Never.

—But what will you do?

—I'll build a hut here and live in it.

—But they'll come and take you away, Horse. You heard Harkins what he said, that he'd send you to Artane.

—Too old, Horse grunted.

The boy looked at the knife in his hand, shaping silent words on his lips, testing them. He said:

—They might put you in prison.

Horse turned, the axe held loosely by his side. His pale blue eyes were wide, his mouth worked uncertainly.

—They won't put me away anywhere, he muttered. They come for me here, I'll show them.

He whirled about and with a grunt brought the axe down savagely into the fork where two long branches met. They split apart with a crack, one fell on either side, torn and dead. He moved on into the tree, the axe flashing as he swung it again and again, white chunks of wood flying about him.

The boy watched the wood falling and flying, the axe flashing, and Horse's mouth moving mutely, and thought he heard, far away in the wood, other sounds of destruction echoing these about him. At last Horse's axe embedded itself in the trunk of the tree, and he grew calm as he worked it loose.

After a long time the boy said quietly:

—I saw someone in the wood.

The wind rattled the leaves above them.

—In the trees out by the fire, he said. I thought someone was moving around and watching me.

Horse stared at him with his mouth open, then he turned and crashed away through the trees toward the clearing where the fire burned. Alone now, the boy looked at the branch in his hands, bare of its bark and gleaming like a moist bone. He raised his eyes and looked fearfully into the shadows gathering about him, and listened to the stirrings and rustlings. He stood up and went out to the fire. Horse was sitting on his heels among the leaves, carefully feeding the flames with pieces of dry wood. The boy sat down beside him.

—Did you see anyone?

Horse shook his head absently. His eyes were vague, as though his mind were moving in some private landscape. They sat silent, listening to the small voice of the fire singing. The rain stopped, and in its place the night began to fall. The boy said:

—Maybe I only imagined there was someone.

Horse was biting his knuckles and gazing pensively into the fire. The red flames flashed in his eyes.

—How could you live here, Horse, in the cold and wet? the boy asked. And you know they'd come and get you. They'd come for you and then they'd say you were mad and put you away. What would you do then?

Horse pushed another stick into the flames.

—They wouldn't get me. I'd be gone before they came. Run away.

The boy sighed and rubbed his forehead.

—All right, Horse. But maybe we should go home just for tonight. Just until you have everything fixed up here.

—I'm not going home.

He began to rock slowly on his heels. A long tongue of flame leaped in the fire. The boy shivered as the damp ground sent a chill along his spine. Horse said:

—I had a white rabbit one time. She had pink eyes and a pink snout. She was a nice rabbit. I kept her in a hutch I made with chicken wire and all. Something got in at her one night and killed her. Ripped her throat like that—slash. Like that.

He paused, and turned his great pale eyes on the boy.

—They won't find me.

And then, as though his challenge had been heard, there came to them the sounds of something moving through the wood. Horse got to his feet and stood with the axe held in his fist. The boy looked up at his face, searching for a sign. The noises came nearer, and then a figure left the trees and came slowly toward the light.

Horse raised the axe, and the flames flashed along the wicked cutting edge. He took a step forward, and another, and the figure before him halted in uncertainty. All was still. Far off in the wood something cried out, and the strange voice called to them over the tops of the dark trees.

—What's up, Horse? said the figure in the shadows. It's me.

Horse gave a grunt of surprise, and the boy jumped to his feet.

—Rice, he cried. You gave us a fright, boy you really did.

Startled at the loudness of his own voice, he lowered his head and looked at his hands in confusion. Rice advanced, and Horse lowered the axe but did not move from where he stood. Rice passed him by, laughing nervously.

—You gave me a bigger fright, he said. Your man there with the hatchet, I thought he was going to take my head off.

He laughed again, and stood by the fire with his hands on his hips. Horse came and sat by them without a word. Rice looked from one of them to the other and asked:

—What's up here?

—Nothing, said the boy. Why?

—You're very pale, the two of you. Who did you think I was, anyway?

—Why did you come out here? Horse asked quietly.

—Do you not like my company, Mr Big Shot?

Horse shrugged his shoulders and looked away. Rice turned and grinned at the boy, and winked. Rice was a fat little boy with a plump round face and straw-coloured hair. He had short thick fingers with broken nails, and he was always short of breath. He turned to Horse again and said:

—You're getting dangerous with that hatchet. Some day you'll go rightly off your nut and brain somebody.

He gave a little wheezing laugh. Rice was the only one of the gang who was not awed by Horse. Now he said:

—Hey Horse.

—What?

—I have a message for you. I came out with it specially.

—What message?

—Ah let it wait a while, Rice said slyly.

He slipped his hand into his pocket and drew out a sticky pink sweet and popped it into his mouth. Sucking noisily, he gazed into the fire.

—Funny thing, he said. I met a fellow out on the road.

They looked up at him, waiting, but he seemed to have forgotten about them. He brooded, his cheeks working slowly on the sweet, and then the boy prompted:

—Well? What about it?

Rice looked down at him, startled.

—What about what?

—The fellow you met.

—O yes. Yes.

He sat down between them, taking great care that his bottom was covered by the tail of his raincoat.

—Well, he said. I was coming up the hill on the bike and it was getting dark. There was this fellow sitting in the ditch at the top. Well, I wasn't afraid of him or anything, but as I said it was getting dark, like. Anyway, when I was going past him he calls me over and tells me about this murder.

He paused, and the silence about them seemed to grow more intense. After a moment Rice went on:

—He said there was a woman killed in town last night. Her head was battered in.

—What woman? Horse asked, without raising his head.

—That Mrs Hanlon that had the shop in the lane down by the picture house. You know her. We used to get the sweets from her when the matinees were on. Her.

—I know her, the boy said. I remember her.

—This fellow, anyway, he said that she wasn't found until this evening. She was on the floor behind the counter and the shop was shut. She was on the floor and her head battered in and blood everyplace.

—Who did it? the boy asked.

Rice ignored him. He was staring into the fire with a perplexed look.

—He was a funny guy, he murmured.

—Who?

—This fellow that said about her getting murdered. Funny-looking.

—But who did the murder, Rice?

—What? O I don't know. He said that no one knew. The guards are looking for a man but he says they won't find him. He says anyone who'd do a thing like that would be smart enough not to get caught. He was a queer guy.

Horse moved a little away from them, and with his axe began to cut a notch in a thick green branch. Rice and the boy stared into the fire.

—Nothing was took, Rice said.

—What do you mean?

—He said there was nothing took out of the shop. No money or anything. Nothing at all. That's queer, isn't it?

—Queer all right.

The boy looked at the wood that encircled them. It was fully dark now, and the firelight threw long shadows that pranced and leaped against the trees. He shivered, and turned to Horse. But Horse was gone.

—Horse, he called softly, but no answer came.

Rice stood up and looked about him.

—Where's that mad eejit gone to now. I never heard him make a move.

They stood side by side and peered into the darkness that lay between the trees. They looked at each other uneasily. The boy crossed the clearing to where Horse had been sitting. No trace was left of him but the branch he had been whittling, it lay there in the firelight with a deep wound in its side, bleeding a trickle of sap.

—Hey, Rice softly called to him. Look at this.

The boy went and stood beside him and looked where he pointed. Horse's axe lay at their feet, a wicked weapon among the leaves. They turned and walked slowly together about the perimeter of the clearing. They searched the shadows, and even stepped among the trees, but would go no deeper than where the firelight reached. They called to him, and called, and nothing answered but the wild wood's echo.

LOVERS

Birds were going mad in the square, spring and the recent rain had them convinced that they were enchanters. Muriel crossed the road and sauntered along by the green railings, swinging her bag and whistling with the magic music. Late April sunlight was in the street, softly washing against the houses and dusting the ragged trees with colour.

She turned the corner and light from above flashed in her eyes. She looked along the tall face of the houses. At a high open window a figure stood, one hand on the sill. She waved her arm, and smiling she lowered her head and ran across the road. As she came near it the door opened and a bent old man in a shabby raincoat shuffled out on the step. He peered at her, his jaw working, his little eyes half closed against the light. She was about to step past him when he turned and slowly, firmly closed the door. She watched him as he went down the steps muttering to himself, then she grinned and put out her tongue at his back. She rang the bell. After a long moment she heard steps in the hall, and Peter opened the door.

—Well, she said. You came at last.

He stood in the dark musty hall, smiling, one arm raised and laid along the edge of the door. The front of his sweater was covered in dust, and he needed a shave. He was about to speak when she pointed at his head and laughed.

—Look at you, she said. You have cobwebs in your hair.

—Cobwebs. So I have.

They climbed the stairs and he put his arm around her and kissed her cheek. She said:

—Have you everything ready?

—Almost.

The flat looked as though something had exploded there. On the sagging bed were piled books and papers tied into bundles with thick white string. Two battered trunks stood by the window, their straps straining. The kitchen table held the remnants of two or three meals, and the floor had a thick layer of dust that soaked the sunlight where it fell. An ancient wardrobe lay on its side before the fireplace like a great dead animal, its mirror smashed. She stood in the middle of it all and looked around with comic despair. He lit a cigarette and leaned his long thin frame against the sideboard. He watched her, smiling. She said:

—Have we to take all this?

—Well, not the wardrobe.

She laughed, and dropping her bag she stepped near him, and the light picked out the tiny yellow flecks in the pupils of her eyes. When she opened her lips a thin silver thread hung between them an instant, and broke. He took her in his arms and kissed her. After a moment she laid her cheek against his neck and asked:

—What will we do today, Peter?

He did not answer, but buried his face in her dark hair. She moved back a pace and looked up at him.

—What's wrong?

—Nothing, he murmured. Have you forgotten?

—What?

—We said we'd visit my father. You said you would come with me.

She went to the window, and he said wearily to her back:

—One day. It's not much.

—I know. But I'm afraid of him, Peter.

He snapped his teeth together and looked at the floor. He said:

—How can you say that? He's just an old man.

—I don't know.

He went to her, and her lip was trembling when she turned. He took her face in his hands. At first she would not look at him, but he stood silently and stared at her until she raised her eyes. He said slowly:

—He's an old man and dying and he can't touch us even if he wanted to. Next week we shall be in France and then the world is before us. There's nothing to fear.

She dropped her eyes again, murmuring:

—I know. I know. But Peter, I'm not logical like you and . . . and strong.

He laughed suddenly, and putting his arms around her he picked her up and whirled her in a circle. With her hands on his shoulders she looked down at him and giggled. He buried his face between her breasts and shouted:

—We're getting out. Out. Away.

He set her down again and said into her face, his voice shaking with laughter:

—You hear me, you mad bitch? We're getting out and we're not coming back. Think of it.

With her mouth open she grinned, nodding her head, yes, yes.

—And we'll be free, she said.

—We'll be free. We're young and the world is wide. We'll be free.

He told her to wait then, and whistling gaily he left the flat. She listened to his steps fade down the stairs, and when the whistling too had faded she turned back to the window and put her face against the glass. The sun-drenched street was empty but for a lame dog that stood in the gutter, sniffing delicately at a soiled scrap of newspaper. From far off came the sound of faint music, beating softly through the air with slow, sad strokes. The dog lifted a leg and watered on the paper, shook himself, and trotted away. The music ceased, and there was silence. Muriel turned and stood with her arms stiff by her sides and looked at the disordered flat, the books, the dust, the blue threads of smoke he had left to hang so still on the air. Everything seemed strange, and somehow mournful, as though the things she knew were fading into the past even as she stood there. She began to weep.

When he came back she was standing before the mirror, painting her eyelids. He stopped whistling and looked closely at her reflection in the glass.

—You've been crying.

—I have not. Where were you?

—At the shop. Why were you crying?

—I wasn't. I told you I wasn't.

—All right. You wasn't.

She twisted about and fell into his arms, pulling him close. She said:

—Everything will be all right, Peter, won't it?

—Of course. Now let's go see the man.

She went out of the flat, and on the stairs Peter kissed her again and told her that everything would be fine.

By the canal the green bus carried them, past the hideous new buildings of glass and steel, past bored swans, the dusty trees, past the old men who walked the tow paths to watch the water in its changes. Peter said:

—I wonder if we'll miss all this.

She looked at the streets riding past.

—I will. I'll miss it. Poor city.

The trees were in bloom in the grounds of the hospital, their faint wood perfumes mingled with the smell of cut grass. As they walked up the drive a pair of pigeons fled before them, their wings clattering in the silence. Cars were parked before the entrance, and a withered old lady was slowly picking her way across the lawn.

They went in through the high doors and stopped at the reception desk, where a nurse with a bored expression sat behind the glass. From the stairs above them came the sound of voices to disturb the hanging silence.

—Mr Williams, please, Peter said.

The nurse looked slowly from one of them to the other, then lowered her eyes and examined Muriel's white linen dress. She ran her finger down a chart before her on the desk and said:

—Three-forty-two. The corridor to your right. Count the doors.

They walked down the white echoing corridor. Far off at the end there was a window of frosted glass where the sun came in and made a mist of light that glared on the polished floor. Muriel pulled down the corners of her mouth and said in a funereal voice:

—Count the doors, all ye who enter here.

Peter smiled vaguely at her and looked away. They came to the room and he knocked gently.

The walls were of the same sterile white as the corridor, and the floor had pale green tiles. There was a plywood wardrobe and a small locker. Opposite the door a square window looked out over the lawn to the trees along the drive. The bed was long and narrow, with white enamelled legs and a white spread. The old man lay there propped up against the pillows, his face turned to the window.

—Hello dad, Peter said.

Slowly the old man turned his head and looked at them blankly. Muriel took time to close the door, then stood awkwardly with her weight on one leg. The old man was tiny, his feet reached only half way down the bed. His thin hair was white as the walls, and his eyes were small and dim and seemed to look inward. His withered hands lay motionless on the covers like two white, plucked birds. He continued to gaze at them without sign of recognition. Peter rubbed his hands on his trousers, and laughed nervously and said:

—It's me. Peter. How are you today, dad?

Without a word the old man turned back to the window. Peter signalled with his eyes to Muriel, and she sat down carefully on the end of the bed. She said brightly:

—Hello Mr Williams. It's Muriel. Don't you remember me?

The old man looked at her and calmly said:

—I remember you.

His voice was surprising, strong and deep, a heavy man's voice. It was all that remained of his youth.

—I'm glad, she muttered weakly, and looked down at her fingers worrying the clasp of her bag. Peter put his hand on her shoulder. He said:

—You look well, dad. How are they treating you here?

The old man smiled faintly and said:

—Their kindness is proportional to the size of one's fee. They show me great kindness. I should have stayed at home.

Peter sat on the bed at the other side from Muriel and wound his long legs about each other. The old man looked at him without expression and asked:

—Where is your mother?

Peter opened his mouth helplessly and said nothing. The old man went on:

—She should come to see me. It's not asking a great deal of her. Tell her she must come.

—Yes dad. I'll tell her.

The old man leaned forward and peered closely at his son.

—You look unhappy, he barked. What is it?

—Nothing, dad. I'm happy.

—So you should be. You have a life.

There was silence. From outside came the *snip-snip* of shears. The old man sighed, and his hands fluttered restlessly. Peter said:

—We're leaving on Monday.

The old man said nothing for a moment, and Peter glanced at Muriel. She was still looking at her hands, but she was faintly smiling now.

—This is the last time you will see me then, the old man said.

Peter laughed uneasily.

—Why do you say that?

—Because it's true.

His dim eyes turned swiftly and settled on Muriel. Loudly he asked:

—Are you going with my son, young lady?

—What?

She looked up quickly and glanced at Peter, who said:

—Yes, dad, Muriel is coming with me.

The old man murmured sourly:

—Has she no voice?

Muriel lifted her head and shook a strand of hair away from her forehead. With her eyes narrowed she stared at the old man.

—Yes, I'm going away too. Peter and I are going away together.

The old man shrugged his shoulders, and the faint shadow of a smile came back to his face. He said:

—She has a voice.

Peter shifted on the bed, took out a cigarette and put it away again. He locked his fingers together and said:

—We'll come back at the end of the year to see you, dad.

Muriel turned and stared at him, but he had turned with his back to her. She opened her mouth to speak but the old man was there before her.

—I shall be dead by then.

Peter rubbed his forehead and said:

—Don't talk like that, dad. Why, you'll outlive us all.

The old man stared at him and said coldly:

—Since when do you think I need to hear that kind of nonsense? I shall be dead before the year is out. And glad of it. I've seen enough of this world. I want to . . .

He paused, and a shadow settled in his eyes. He blinked rapidly and went on:

—I want to go home.

Peter lifted his eyes to the window.

—Home? he murmured, puzzled.

The old man followed his son's gaze to the window, to the trees and the soft sunlight. He said:

—I've lived too long. These last years have been useless. They have kept me going with needles and drugs and pills, and for what? To see everything slip away and die. Now you are going too and I have nothing. Even your mother won't visit me.

Peter looked at him and said evenly:

—Dad, you know mother is dead.

—Do I need to be told that?

Again his eyes wandered to the window.

—When we were young we used to walk up here. Fields then. Nothing but fields. The city was smaller. It was easy to live and we thought we would live forever. But everything dies. I've lost two wives. I've seen too many deaths and now all I live for is to see my own.

Suddenly he turned to them, and his little eyes were bright. He clasped his hands together and said briskly:

—You're going away.

—Yes.

—When?

—Monday we—

—Where?

—France first and then—

—How will you live?

—Well, we'll . . . we'll find things as we go along. Fruit picking or—anyway I have a little money.

The old man nodded once, and gave a long sigh. He leaned back against the pillows and after a moment he said quietly:

—You have my money.

Peter looked at him, and his forehead wrinkled.

—How do you mean, dad?

—I sent instructions yesterday that you were now solely in charge of my affairs.

—What does that mean?

Muriel leaned across the bed toward Peter. There was apprehension in her eyes. She clutched his hand, but he did not look at her. The old man glanced in her direction and said:

—Be quiet, girl. Now, my boy, I shall tell you what it means. You are from now head of the firm of Williams and Son.

Peter's mouth was open as he stared at his father. There was a long silence. At last Peter said:

—But I am going away, dad.

The old man waved a hand.

—The business runs itself. You may take your holiday. It means merely that you will now be rich enough to enjoy it.

—But dad . . .

—Well?

—I don't know. This is all very—

Muriel struck his wrist with her knuckles, and he turned to her in surprise. She said slowly:

—We're going away, Peter.

He smiled, and as though explaining to a child he said:

—Yes, of course, Muriel. You heard dad saying we could go.

—That's not what he said, and you know it.

They stared at each other, and the old man watched them, the thin smile on his lips. He said to her quietly:

—Everything dies, my dear. Everything.

Without looking at him she stood up and walked stiffly to the door.

—Where are you going? Peter called.

She paused with her hand on the door, but did not turn.

—I'm going, she said.

And was gone. Peter turned to his father, and the old man said innocently:

—The young lady seems upset. I wonder why.

—I don't know.

The old man picked at the sheet, his lips pursed. After a moment he said:

—Peter, I think I may have exaggerated a little. Head of the firm—a figure of speech, you understand. But you have the money, which I suppose at this stage is what matters. Anyway, the business would bore a young man. Am I right?

—I suppose so, dad.

Peter uncoiled himself from the bed.

—I think I better follow her. You'll take care of yourself until we get back.

—Of course.

He went to the door, and there the old man's voice stopped him:

—But you won't be going away now, will you?

—Why do you say that?

He pulled the sheets an inch nearer his chin and folded his hands again over his stomach. He said:

—I shall live a little longer, now.

Peter went out into the corridor. With the door almost closed he stopped and looked back at his father through the narrow opening. The old man was smiling to himself. When he turned to the door, Peter quickly closed it, but not before he heard:

—And bring your mother with you next time, boy.

Outside the hospital Muriel stood and watched the gardener cutting down the dead stalks of flowers. When Peter came up she did not move or speak. He said peevishly:

—Why did you run out like that? He is my father, after all.

—I'm sorry, she said in a flat voice.

They turned and started down the drive. He glanced at her from the corner of his eye and said:

—I think we'll have to wait a week or two now before we go. This changes things.

—Yes.

They moved slowly between the smooth lawns. The afternoon was ending. In the trees the birds were going mad.

A DEATH

They lowered the coffin into the grave, and Stephen turned away his face. He watched idly a small, fat man who moved with curious stealth along the perimeter of the dark yew trees. Far in the distance the sea was swollen and rough, and dotted with flecks of white. A cold wind came from the north, carrying with it a few small drops of rain. The little man had halted, and now stood motionless against the restless trees, staring fixedly across the headstones at the bedraggled groups of mourners. Stephen looked back to the grave. They were watching him, he tried to weep, but he had no tears. Beside him Alice sobbed, and that seemed ironic. She had hated the old man. He frightened her, or so she said.

The ceremony ended and they moved away from the grave.

—How do you feel? Alice asked. Are you all right?

—Yes. Fine. I'm glad it's over now.

He put his arm around her shoulders as she stumbled through the thick damp grass. She had not even yet become accustomed to her pregnancy. The wind blew in the trees and rattled the branches as if they were hung with bones. He shivered, and said:

—Let's get out of this place.

They began to walk faster, but when they came to the main path Alice's steps faltered, and she hung back, murmuring:

—O my God . . .

He looked where she was looking, and saw coming toward them the fat little man who had stood in the trees behind the grave. He wore a dusty black overcoat that reached well past his knees. His head was completely bald, and on the back of it a hat, too small for him, sat crookedly. As he hurried along on his little legs he cast frightened glances to right and left. He stopped before them and leaned close with an air of conspiracy. The rain was releasing from his coat a dull faint smell.

—Stephen, he breathed. My sympathy.

Stephen took the offered hand and glanced uneasily at his wife. She stood with downcast eyes, tightly clutching her gloves.

—Such a wonderful old person, Stephen, the little man said, gazing up at him with intense bright eyes. As you know, I knew him well and it was such a shock to see him go like that so suddenly. Dear me, such a shock. Indeed yes.

—I'm sorry, Stephen said. I don't seem to remember—

—Come, the little man interrupted him. I'll walk with you to your car.

He stepped between them with a neat little hop. With protection now on either side of him he lost his furtive air. Stephen looked over the top of the bald pate between them at his wife, signalling frantically with his eyes, but she would not look at him. The little man said:

—You know, sometimes I feel that a whole race is passing. Certainly, Stephen, your father is an example. Not just a generation mind, but, yes, a whole race. Don't you agree?

Stephen said nothing, and the little man turned to the wife.

—Don't you agree with me, Alice?

She stared at him in fright and said:

—What? Yes. O yes.

Stephen glanced at her, but she had retreated again, her hand to her mouth.

—Ah yes, a whole race, the little man said with satisfaction. It will be a great loss when they are all gone. What has this new generation to offer the world? Only the fruits of their fear.

After a little silence Stephen said stiffly:

—I don't see how the world can be made any worse.

The little man looked up at him from under his eyebrows, slyly smiling.

—But there are so many new evils, he said softly.

Stephen coughed.

—Surely there are no new ones.

But the little man was gazing away out at the ugly sea, lost in thought. Suddenly he started.

—What say? Pardon?

—I said—I said surely there are no new evils. You said—

—Ah yes yes yes. We're told there can be nothing new, yes, but look at the things that have happened these last few years. Terrible. Terrible indeed. Sometimes I think that—that—what was I saying?

He was becoming agitated, and was looking about him again in fear. Stephen watched him with puzzled eyes. He went on:

—There is a new brand of despair in the world. The old ways are dying, and the old religion too. When people turn their backs on God what can they expect? What can they expect, I say?

He looked at them with his bright, troubled eyes.

—I know, he said. I turned my back on God. I wanted to serve him. The call was there, the call to serve, but I told myself it led to death. I was proud and now I have nothing.

They reached the car.

—I have nothing left.

Stephen opened the door for his wife and she got hurriedly inside.

—Without God nothing. Do you hear me?

He put his hand on Stephen's arm, and Stephen tried to push it away, but the fat little fingers held him.

—Do you know what I'm talking about, do you? Have you seen the terror and felt the angel of death brush your face with his wing? Have you?

His eyes were wide now with a fixed stare, and there were spots of white on his mouth. Stephen said with difficulty, looking anxiously to see if the people in the other cars were watching:

—Look, I don't know who you are.

—Have you seen it, I say? Have you?

—Listen . . .

—Admit it. Admit that everywhere you look is desolation. The hand of a spurned god has touched the world and still we ignore it. I tell you, that same hand will touch us with only death unless we—

—Let go of my arm.

—Admit it. Only admit it.

—You're mad.

Abruptly the little man relaxed, and the brightness went from his eyes. It was as though he had been awaiting this accusation. Quietly he said:

—Mad. Indeed. I saw the horror and the desolation but I

would not call it by its name. I had no courage or not enough. If I'm mad it's that failure that drove me to it. But you. You could if you chose, you could—

—Shut up, Stephen cried. Shut your mouth you old fool and get away from me. Get away.

He pushed the little man off, and his ill-fitting hat slipped from his head and rolled in the gravel. He came back again, his finger outstretched, his lips wet. Stephen got into the car and slammed the door. While he started the engine the little man came near and pressed his face against the window. He stared at them silently with his burning eyes. Stephen forced the gears, and the tyres screamed as the car fled away down the drive.

They came to the road that led to the village. Stephen was shaking and he said between his teeth:

—Madman. Jesus.

Alice said nothing, and he turned and looked at her sharply. He asked:

—Who was he?

She shrugged her shoulders.

—But you knew him, he said.

—What makes you think that?

—You recognised him, he insisted. You stopped on the path when you saw him coming.

—Does that mean I knew him? she asked, regarding him calmly.

Stephen was confused. He looked out at the road and muttered:

—He knew us. He knew our names. Who the hell was he? This is a small place, I grew up here. I should know him.

For a time there was silence, and then he muttered:

—These bloody lunatics should all be locked up.

—He was sad.

—Sad? Sad? He was a lunatic.

—But he was still sad. Why are you so cruel?

—Cruel, you say? Did you hear the things he said to me? Don't talk rot.

—I'm not talking rot.

—He was a complete head-case and it was obvious to everyone but you. Did you see how no one would come near us when they saw him there? Did you see that? Yes. They bloody well knew, but of course Alice with her gentility and kindness would say nothing but just stand there and let me walk right into it like a fool. Jesus.

—O stop it, for god's sake. I told you I didn't know him.

She covered her ears and began to rock back and forth in her seat. He said:

—I'm sorry.

—That's all you can ever say.

He cast agonized eyes at the roof.

—Jesus, Alice, don't start. It's been a rough day and I've had all I can take. Please don't start.

She sat upright and rubbed her eyes. Lighting a cigarette she said:

—We started long ago.

—Alice . . .

—Leave me alone.

Beside him the evening fields flowed silently, swiftly past. The day was fading now, and the trees were full of darkness.

—Do you want to go home tonight? he asked, and tried to make it sound like an apology.

—I don't mind.

Her voice was cold, and held a world of weariness. He made a noise with his teeth and said:

—I was going to write a book one time. Did you know that?

She looked at him in surprise.

—No, I didn't.

He laughed.

—O yes, I was going to write a book. A love story. The story of Stephen and Alice who thought that love would last forever. And when they found that it wouldn't or at least that it changed so much that they couldn't recognise it anymore, the blow was too heavy. They retreated into themselves like rabbits into a burrow.

He stopped, and she sighed.

—You're too cruel, she murmured. Too cruel.

When they came into the kitchen Lilian was by the table, bent over a cup of tea. She did not look at them. Stephen watched her, his only sister, as he took off his scarf and gloves. She was growing old, there were wrinkles at the corners of her eyes, and grey in her hair. The old man's death had wounded her deeply. Now she would have no one to care for and bully in her ineffectual way.

—Is there any tea? Alice asked, struggling out of her coat. She blew her nose.

—In the pot, Lilian answered, lifting a listless hand.

Stephen left the room and the two women together in their silence. He was washing his hands in the bathroom when Alice tapped on the door.

—Steve, I'm going to lie down for a while. I'm tired.

—Yes. A rest will do you good. You'll have to take it easy now until the baby comes.

She leaned against the door, pale and drab, running a damp knotted handkerchief through her fingers.

—I think we'll go back tonight, she said.

—Are you sure you're up to it?

—Maybe you're right. It's been a long day.

—We'll wait until morning, then.

—Yes.

When she had gone he went down again to the kitchen. Lilian was standing by the sink. She looked at him and opened her mouth to speak, but instead she looked away.

—Alice looks pale, she said after a moment.

—Yes. She's tired. This has all been a strain on her.

—On all of us.

—Yes.

She stored the cups and saucers in the cupboard, then dried her hands and said:

—I have to feed the hens.

—Lilian, he began, and stopped. She stood with her head bent, waiting. He went on awkwardly:

—You'll be lonely now.

She shrugged her shoulders, and blushed. He said:

—I was thinking, Lily, that maybe—maybe you'd like to come up and stay with us for a few days. It would take you out of yourself. This place—this is no place for a woman to live on her own.

—I might, she said doubtfully. I suppose I could manage it.

She glanced at him from under her eyebrows and smiled, a nervous, girlish smile. Then in confusion she fled out into the yard.

He wandered restlessly about the room. The strange clarity of vision and thought which follows exhaustion now came over him. The things around him as he looked at them began to seem unreal in their extreme reality. Everything he touched gave to his fingers the very essence of itself. The table seemed to vibrate in the grains of its wood, the steel of the sink was cold and sharp as ice. It was as if he were looking down from a great height through some mysterious spiral. In the corner behind the stove a blackthorn stick leaned against the wall. When he saw it he stepped forward and put out his fingers to touch it, but halted, frowning. He stared at the knots, and they seemed to be whirling in the dark wood, each one a small, closed world. He moved back uncertainly, and dropped his hand. Then he turned and quickly left the room.

He went upstairs to the small bedroom that looked out over the yard to the fields beyond the house. Alice lay on the bed among the shadows, fitfully dozing. Her hands were clasped over her swollen stomach. From the window he looked down into the yard. Lilian stood among the chickens, throwing food to them from her apron. The clucking of the birds came faintly to his ears. The last light was dying, soon it would be night. He stood with his forehead against the glass and gazed out over the darkening fields to the dark hills in the distance.

—Stephen? came Alice's drowsy, querulous voice. He turned to her, saying:

—Did I wake you? I'm sorry.

—It doesn't matter.

He sat beside her on the bed. She lifted her arm and touched his cheek with a damp palm. He sighed.

—What is it? she asked.

—I don't know. I was thinking about father. I don't seem to . . . I don't . . .

He stopped, and lifted his hands in a helpless gesture.

—All I can remember is his knuckles. They were white, you know, and they used to curl around his stick—like that. Imagine your father being dead two days and all you can remember is a little thing like that. Today at the grave I couldn't cry. I wanted to, but I couldn't. I looked at the coffin and it didn't seem to have anything to do with me.

—It's the shock, she said.

He stood up with his hands in his pockets and paced the room. Frowning at the floor he said:

—I loved him. I know I did.

—Of course.

—Then what happened to that love is what I want to know? How did it die so easily? I loved him more than anything in the world.

He stopped and looked down at her, asking:

—How does love just die like that, Alice?

She said:

—Things kill it.

He stared at her. She bit her lip, as though she knew she had said too much and was afraid of saying more.

—What things? he asked, apprehension rising through his words.

—I don't know.

—Look at me, Alice. What things?

But her eyes skittered away from his like frightened animals. She touched her face with agitated fingers.

—I don't know anything about it, she cried. Why do you ask me? Why? Things just do—terrible things.

He sat beside her again, and stared at his hands clasped before him.

—You're lying, he said, frowning. You're talking nonsense. That is all . . . this . . . I know this is all wrong.

He stared down at her, but she had shut her eyes.

—It's all wrong, he said again, shaking his head.

For a time all was still. Faint sounds came to him, the clucking of the chickens in the yard, the small winds singing in the slates. He laid his hand gently on the rise of her stomach. She gave a little moan, and turned her face to the wall, and as she did he felt the strange child move beneath his hand.

THE VISIT

—It's going to rain, the old woman said. Pull up your hood.

She took the girl's hand. Before them, at the top of the crooked field, the roof of the house shone in the light and three trees stood against the sky. It was the first day of spring and the wind from the mountains blew cold and clear, and shadows raced across the fields. They came to the lane behind the house and the old woman stopped to rest. The girl looked out at the distant sea, and the wind lifted her long yellow hair. A damp gust rattled the trees, and drops of rain flashed in the sunlight. Close by there was the sound of water falling over stones, and a thrush suddenly whistled.

—Tantey, said the girl. Why are there seasons?

The old woman looked at her startled.

—What sort of question is that?

In the kitchen the stove roared and the wind in the chimney blew the smoke back into the room. The old woman grumbled to herself as she struggled out of her cape. She gave it to the girl to hang behind the door and hobbled across and sat in the chair. The girl went to the window and looked out over the fields. The sound of the wind made her feel restless and vaguely excited, and she wanted to go out again and run madly through the grass. Behind her the old woman said:

—What are you at there?

—Nothing. Just looking out.

She went and sat on the arm of the chair beside her aunt.

—When will papa be here, Tantey?

The old woman did not answer. She fumbled in the pocket of her black dress.

—Where are my sweets? she muttered. Now I put them here, I'm sure of it.

The girl went to the dresser and brought back the grimy bag of peppermints.

—Ah you're a good girl, the old woman said.

She sucked her sweet, nodding and staring blankly at her hands. After a while she looked up at the girl and smiled and gently pulled her hair.

—Your papa is a fine man, she said.

—But when is he coming?

—Maybe after tea, she snapped. Have patience.

The girl stood up and walked to the window, twisting her fingers. With her mouth set in a sulky line she muttered:

—I'm fed up waiting. I don't think he's coming at all. I think he's forgot all about me.

The old woman smacked her hands together.

—Stop that talk. Forgot you indeed, and how could your own father forget you? You should be ashamed, carrying on like a baby.

The girl ran back and sat on the floor beside the chair. She licked her finger and rubbed the dried blood from a scratch on her knee. She said:

—Tell me about him again, Tantey.

—Well. He's very tall and straight and—O he carries himself like that.

She pushed back her shoulders and held up her head at a proud and arrogant tilt. Then suddenly she gave a cackle of laughter and began to rock back and forth in her chair. She leaned down and ruffled the girl's hair.

—O he's like a prince out of a story book, she cried, and her eyes closed up completely she laughed so hard. Like a prince he is.

—Is he, Tantey? said the girl, smiling uncertainly and watching the old woman's face. And will he like me when he comes? What will he say to me? Will he take me away?

The old woman threw up her hands.

—So many questions. You'll just have to wait and see. Now go and comb your hair and tidy yourself up a bit in case he comes and finds you looking like a little tinker.

Sighing, the girl stood up and went into the dim passage that led to the front of the house. The dining-room was full of moist yellow sunlight that fell on the table and against the walls. She knelt on the couch and put her elbows on the window sill. The wind beat on the glass with a dull sound. Outside, the sun threw up a dazzling reflection from the road. For a long time she stayed there, while shadows came across the fields and leaped against the window. Her eyelids began to droop, but suddenly she lifted her head and pressed her face to the glass. Someone was cycling down the road, a vague dark shape moved on the glistening tar. She went out to the hall, and into the garden, where the wind beat fiercely on her face and shook out her long curls. She stopped outside the gate and shaded her eyes with her hand. The traveller, backpedalling, came across the road in a graceful arc and stopped.

—Well well, he said. What have we here then?

He looked at her, his head to one side, and with his lips

pursed he stepped down from the bicycle and brushed at the wrinkles in his trousers. He was a very tiny man, smaller even than the girl, with a great square head and thick hands. His hair was oiled and carefully parted, and his eyebrows were as black and shiny as his hair. There were four buttons in his jacket, all fastened. At his neck he wore a gay red silk scarf. He said:

—My name is Rainbird.

With her mouth open she stared at him. He watched her and waited for a reply, and when none came he shrugged his shoulders and began to turn away. She said quickly:

—Is that your last name?

He looked around at her, and with his eyebrows arched he said:

—That is my only name.

—O.

He slipped his hands into the pockets of his jacket with his thumbs outside and took a few swaggering turns before the gate.

—Do you live in there? he asked casually, nodding toward the house.

—Yes, she said. That's my house.

He looked up at the ivy-covered walls, at the windows where the lowering sun shone on the glass.

—I lived in a house like that before I went on the road, he said. Much bigger than that it was, of course. That was a long time ago.

—Was it around here?

—Eh?

—Was it around here you lived?

He gave her a pitying look.

—Naw. It was in another country altogether.

The suggestion that he came from these parts seemed to offend him deeply. There was a silence, and then he whirled about and said:

—I can tell fortunes.

—Can you?

With his eyes closed he nodded proudly.

—Yes. Do you want me to tell yours?

She pushed out her hand. He took her fingers with a sly grin, and the tip of his little red tongue came out and explored the corner of his mouth. Then he wiped away the grin, and with great seriousness he bent over her hand. After a moment he stepped back, and with vaguely troubled eyes he considered the sky.

—Well? she asked.

He folded his arms and ruminated deeply, a finger supporting his chin.

—Well it's a difficult hand, he said. I'll tell you that for nothing. You're waiting for someone.

She laughed.

—Yes that's right, you're right. My papa is coming to visit me today. How did you know that?

He seemed a little startled, but he quickly covered it up and said:

—You haven't seen him for a long time.

—I never saw him. He went away after I was born because my mother died.

—Yes, he said sagely. Yes.

He clasped his hands behind his back and walked around her in a circle, rolling from side to side on his short bandy legs. At last he stopped and shook his head.

—No, he sighed. I see nothing else. If I had my cards . . .

He looked at the ground, and pulled at his lip with a thumb and forefinger. She waited, and then said in disappointment:

—Is that all?

—That's all. Well I told you, it's a difficult hand. What do you expect?

—Can you do any magic?

—I surely can, he said. Why, that's my job.

—Well do a trick for me then.

—I don't do tricks, he said archly. I perform feats of magic.

—All right then, go on, perform a feat of magic. Go on.

—Take it easy, he said. Take it easy. Just hold on a minute now.

Once again he struck a pose with arms folded and finger under his chin.

—Look, he said, and turned up his hands for her to examine. Nothing there, right? Now wait.

She watched him eagerly. He made fists of his large hands and held them out before him, tightly clenched. He was quite still, concentrating, and suddenly he opened his hands again. In the hollow of each palm there lay a small white object. She stepped forward for a closer look, and cried:

—Eyes! They're eyes!

She reached out to touch them, but he quickly closed his fingers over them.

—O let me see them again, she begged. Please. Let me touch them.

He shook his head.

—Forbidden.

—O please.

He grinned delightedly and shoved his fists into his pockets. Out came the tip of his tongue once again.

—No, he said softly.

—All right then, keep them, see if I care. I bet you had them up your sleeves. Anyway they're not real.

She turned away from him and gave the rear wheel of his bicycle a kick. He pulled the machine away from her and glared at her in outrage.

—Watch what you're doing, he threatened.

He gave her another black look, and with an expert little hop he was in the saddle and away down the hill. She watched him go, biting her lip, and then she galloped after him, crying:

—Wait! Wait!

He stopped, and with one foot to the ground he looked back at her. She came up to him, panting, and said:

—Listen, I'm sorry for kicking your bike.

He said nothing, and she lowered her eyes and fingered the rubber grip on the handlebar.

—Would you . . . she began hesitantly. Would you give me a carry down the road a bit?

He considered this for a moment, and the sly grin crept over his face.

—All right, he said, and giggled.

She pulled herself up and sat on the crossbar, and they bowled away down the road. She glanced over her shoulder at him nervously, and he winked.

They moved swiftly now, the hedges flew past on either side and the tyres threw up water that drenched her legs. She looked into the sky, at the swirling clouds, and the wild wind rushed in her hair.

—*Allez up!* he cried out gaily, and the little girl shrieked with laughter, and plucked the red scarf from around his neck and waved it in the wind. Down they went, and down, faster and faster, until at the bottom of the hill the front wheel began to wobble and when he tried to hold it still the machine twisted and ran wildly across the road to tumble them both in the ditch.

She lay smiling with her face buried in the thick wet grass. A hand pulled at her arm, but she shook it off and pressed herself against the ground. All was quiet now, and somewhere above her a bird was singing.

—Eh, listen, little girl. Are you hurt? Hey.

She turned on her back and looked up at him, her fingers on her lips. She smiled and shook her head.

—I'm all right.

He brushed the grass and flecks of mud from his jacket, and all the while he was looking worriedly about. He began to wipe his shoes with his handkerchief. The girl sat up and took the cloth from him and rubbed at the damp leather. He put his hands on his hips and watched her.

—Now, she said, and gave him back his handkerchief.

He took her hand and helped her to her feet. Hurriedly he retrieved his bicycle from the ditch and wiped the saddle with his sleeve. He paused with his foot on the pedal and turned to look at her. She stood with her hands joined before her, and there were leaves and bits of grass in her hair, and a long streak of mud on her cheek. He put a hand into his pocket.

—Here.

She took the little glass ball from him and looked at it. On one side two dark circles were painted, the pupils of an eye.

—Thank you.

He grinned, showing his yellow teeth, and said:

—They weren't real.

—What harm.

Now he cast another look around, and whispered urgently:

—Listen, you won't say you saw me, will you? I mean you won't say I took you on the bike. I might get into trouble.

She shook her head, and he gave her a wink.

She watched him go away down the road. He did not look back, and soon he was gone around a bend. She turned and walked slowly up the hill. The sun had fallen behind the mountains, and the clouds, like bruised blood, were massing.

Tantey stood in the doorway, and when she saw the little girl come wandering along she cried:

—There you are. Come here to me. Where have you been? And look at the state of you! I should box your ears.

She caught the girl by the shoulder and gave her a shake.

—I went for a walk, the girl muttered sullenly.

—Went for a walk indeed.

She led her down the hall, and to the kitchen. While the girl scrubbed her hands at the sink the old woman fussed about her, straightening her dress and pulling the pieces of leaf from her hair.

—Were you rolling around in the fields or what? An infant wouldn't be the trouble. A nice sight you'll be to greet your papa.

The girl turned from the sink and stared with wide eyes at the old woman.

—Has he come? she asked, and her lip trembled.

—Yes child, he's come. Now tidy yourself up and we'll go in to him.

The girl slowly dried her hands, staring before her thoughtfully. At last she said:

—I don't want to see him.

—What are you saying? Hurry up now.

—I won't go near him.

—Have you lost the bit of sense you had? He's come all the way from London just to see you.

—I don't care.

The old woman stepped forward with her lips shut tight and caught the girl's hair in her hand.

—If you won't come by yourself I'll drag you. Come on and stop this nonsense, you little rip.

She pulled the girl struggling out into the passage and along the hall.

—No Tantey, I don't want to see him! No Tantey, you're hurting me!

The old woman pushed open the door of the dining-room. Inside, the tall grey-haired man was sitting at the table, twisting the brim of his hat in his long fingers.

—No Tantey, no, you're hurting my hair!

The girl clutched at the door frame, tears on her face, while the old woman tugged furiously at her hair. The grey-haired man rose uncertainly and peered out at them with raised eyebrows. When she saw him the girl sent up a fearful wail, and lifting her arm she flung something, something white flashed past him and there was the tinkle of glass breaking. He spoke, but his words were drowned by the cries of the girl:

—No Tantey no, leave me alone, I don't want to see him, I don't want to, you're hurting me, Tantey, let go you're hurting me . . .

SANCTUARY

Julie awoke in the chill October morning to find the air before her face finely traced with a web of blood. In the day's first terror she reached out blindly beside her. The bed was empty. She whimpered, but already the mist had begun to fade from her eyes. She lay back on the pillow and wiped the sweat from her lips, from the hollows of her eyes. On the ceiling above her, light moved and flowed, reflections from the sea below her window. She got out of bed, a hand in her damp hair. She pushed her feet into slippers, untangled a knot in the sash of her nightgown, stood up unsteadily. Another day, the last, another day.

From the bathroom she went down the stairs, buttoning her blouse. She paused on the last step. Helen was in the living room, sitting on the couch by the window, looking out. Light invaded the room through the long window, soft light from the sea, it touched the legs of the table, glowing, and fell among Helen's dark hair. Her hand was raised to her cheek, and in the long white fingers a cheroot burned silently, sending up into the cool sea light a narrow line of smoke. Julie said:

—I dreamed all night of something following me.

Helen did not move, but went on looking toward the beach and the morning sea. Only the silent line of smoke wavered in its course, and then was still again. Julie's eyes narrowed, and her voice was hard when she said:

—And today I'm bleeding. I'm glad this is all finished.

Helen stood up slowly, and slowly turned.

—Why do you say that?

Julie crossed the room and sat down on the couch. Staring at the space between her feet she found a cigarette and fumbled it nervously to her mouth. She left it unlit. Helen looked down at her, faintly smiling, and asked again:

—Why do you say that, Julie?

In the silence both seemed to be pulling on some frail, invisible cord stretched between them. Julie said:

—Where were you when I needed you? Where? You know I can't wake up alone. You know that. You left me there to wake in that awful room with not a sound anywhere. I hate this place.

Helen looked at the cheroot, holding it upright to save the long tip of ash. She said:

—I'm sorry. I didn't think you would wake so early. You don't usually wake so early, do you?

Julie lifted her hands, examined them, and put them away again.

—I have to get out, she said.

Helen went and stood at the window, saying:

—Then you won't come back to university?

—No.

—You mean that? You have decided? You won't take the degree?

—No.

—That will be . . . a pity, Helen said carefully.

Julie closed her eyes and lay back on the couch. After a moment she said in a strange, flat voice, as though reciting a lesson:

—I want to get married. I want to have a baby. My mother worries about me. She asks what are my plans. What are your plans? she asks. What can I tell her? I'm not like you. I'm weak. I feel sorry for her. I want to tell her there's someone. That everything is all right. But what have I to tell her?

She stood up and wandered about the room, turning away from the barrier of each wall with a look of pain.

—Three months we have been here, she said in wonder. Three months and so much has changed. Helen, why do things change?

Helen looked out at the sea. The sun glittered on the water blue as ice. Far out on the sound a flock of gulls was attacking something that floated there, they fell and turned and lifted with the light on their wings, bright birds. Two sails of yachts lay slanted into the wind.

—You will need someone to be there when you wake up, Helen said. You will need someone for that.

—I don't know. Is it cold out today?

—It's a nice day.

—I'll go for a walk. Yes. A walk. My bags are packed.

—Yes. Julie.

—What?

—Will you be coming back to the flat?

—Maybe I'll go away.

There was a pause, and once again Julie spread her hands before her and looked at them absently. She said:

—A degree would be useless to me.

—You were a good pupil, Helen murmured. We got along well.

—It was because you were young. It made a difference to have a young professor.

—But I got through to you.

—Yes.

—I felt that I was getting through to you.

—Yes.

—I'm glad you think that.

—Perhaps I'll go away, Julie said again.

Into the silence between them the small sounds of the sea filtered slowly, the sea which had whispered and sighed through the long nights of the summer. Helen pressed her palms against the glass.

—I'm going for a walk now, Julie said.

Outside, the air struck her like a blade. She walked along the verandah, her sandals knocking on the loose planks, then crossed the tiny garden to the beach. The sand was pockmarked from the night's rain, and near the waves the prints of gulls pointed outward across the sound. A clear, chill wind blew from the islands, carrying against her face the faint perfumes of heather and pine. She looked back to the cottage, at the figure in the dimness of the window watching her, and as she turned a movement on the rocks at the end of the beach caught her eye. A figure, black against the sun, was coming toward her. In the sky above her head a bird screamed, and its shadow brushed her shoulder. The window was empty now. She felt the black claw of terror at her throat, and she turned and ran back across the garden.

The screen door was locked, and she shook it frantically.

—Helen. Helen.

The door opened, and as she stepped quickly inside Helen looked at her with mild curiosity.

—What is it, Julie?

—Nothing. I . . . nothing.

She went into the living room, and Helen followed, watching her. She sat on the couch and squeezed her hands between her knees. Helen stood above her and put a gentle hand on her hair.

—What's wrong, Julie?

—I don't know. Something . . . strange. I saw someone.

—Who did you see?

—Someone. I don't know.

She began to tremble. Helen looked up to the window and slowly smiled.

—Look, Julie. There's who you saw. Look.

Julie turned. Beyond the glass glaring with light someone was moving, a hand was raised, signalling.

—Don't let it in, she breathed, her fingers tearing at each other. Lock the door, Helen.

But Helen was gone. Julie looked away from the window and held her face in her hands. After what seemed a long time she lifted her head, hearing sounds about her.

—Julie. Julie. We have a visitor, Julie, look.

Helen was there before her, smiling, and beside her a stranger.

—Who are you? Julie asked in a small, dead voice.

He was young, not more than eighteen or nineteen, a tall, heavily built boy with a shock of red hair flowing up and away from his forehead. He wore a blue shirt open at the neck, and faded denims. With his hands on his hips he stood and watched her, his wide, handsome face composed and expressionless. He asked:

—Why were you frightened of me, Julie?

She looked from one of them to the other, searching their faces.

—What do you want here? she asked.

—I came to say goodbye to you, he said. You're going away and I came to say goodbye.

She shook her head and looked appealingly at Helen.

—What does he want, Helen?

—He came to say goodbye to us.

—But I don't know him, she wailed.

The boy laughed, and shook the flaming hair away from his forehead. He lit one of Helen's cheroots and sat down on the couch. Julie moved away from him, and he smiled sardonically at her. Helen put her hands on her knees and leaned down to gaze silently into Julie's face. The boy asked:

—Are you sleeping well now, Julie? Do you sleep well?

She did not answer, and he went on:

—Why can't you sleep, Julie?

Again silence. He shrugged his shoulders, and leaving the couch he walked about the room, examining it here and there. Julie followed him with her eyes. Helen reached forward and touched her cheek lightly and then went to stand again at the window. Julie's lips began to move, and she said:

—I'm afraid. I'm afraid of the dark.

The boy stopped in the middle of the floor.

—Well you should leave a light burning. With a light there would be no darkness and then you would not be afraid. Would you?

Julie looked down helplessly at her hands where they lay like dead things in her lap. Without turning, Helen murmured:

—Not that kind of darkness.

—I see, the boy said. Yes I see.

Julie's hands moved, and she smiled at them.

—You see, I'm afraid that I won't wake up and yet I'm afraid of waking too. Sometimes I think there is something in the room. Some animal sitting on its haunches in the corner watching me. And I'm afraid.

The boy ambled out the door, and from the next room he called:

—What kind of animal? In the corner, Julie, what kind of animal is it?

—I don't know, she whispered.

—What? What did you say, Julie?

Helen left the window and sat down in an armchair in the corner. One half of her face now lay in shadow, and Julie looked away from the still, single eye watching her. The boy came back and leaned against the door frame, his arms folded.

—There are some strange things in this house. Shaving lotion. I found shaving lotion.

—I like the perfume, Helen said. I prefer it.

—Ah. You prefer it. But there are other things. In the bathroom.

Helen suddenly laughed, and the sound of her laughter seemed to shake the room. The boy sat again beside Julie. This time she did not move away. She was gazing in a trance at her knees. The boy ran a hand through his hair and said:

—Last year there was a girl here. In this house. She was alone. A very strange girl with blue eyes. I don't think she was Irish. Maybe English. I came to see her. She used to talk too about things following her. Threatening her. I came every day to see her. I listened to her and she said it made her feel better that I listened to her. One day I found her sitting on the floor crying. I asked her what was wrong and she said she was afraid of the sea. I wanted to teach her how to swim and she said that once she could swim and was a strong swimmer but now she had forgotten. She couldn't swim now.

There was silence but for the cries of birds out on the sound. At last Julie asked:

—What happened?

—What?

—The girl. What happened to her? Was she drowned?

—Drowned? No. She went away, I think. But I don't think she was drowned.

Julie stood up and went toward the stairs, her head bent and her arms hanging loosely at her sides.

—Where are you going? Helen said.

—I'm going to . . . to lie down for a little while. Just a little while. I'm so tired. It's strange.

In the bedroom she lay with her hands folded on her breast and listened to their voices. Once they laughed, and in a while all was silence. She watched the reflections of the water above her on the ceiling. They seemed to have but one pattern which constantly formed, dissolved, and reformed again. A small wind came in from the sea and murmured against the window, and the curtains moved with a small scraping sound. Her eyelids fell. She struggled against sleep, but the strange weariness she felt was greater than her fear. She watched in fascinated horror her mind drift into the darkness, floating away with the small sounds of the sea, the distant crying of the birds.

—Helen. Helen.

A voice was screaming, but no call came in answer. The room seemed filled with a white mist that pressed heavily against her eyes. She left the bed and opened the door. A vast, deep silence lay on the house, a silence which seemed to hold in it the inaudible hum of a tremendous machine. She moved to the top of the stairs and sat on the first step. From here she could see into the living room. They were down there, on the couch. She leaned against the banister and watched, listening in awe to the strange sounds, the terrifying sounds. There was a faint warm smell, like the smell of blood and bones. She fled into the bathroom, and there she was sick. When the nausea passed she lowered herself to the floor and leaned her face against the cool enamel of the bath. She wept.

There were footsteps on the stairs, the sound of a door opening quietly, more steps, a voice.

—Julie. What are you doing here?

Crying out, she opened her eyes, then turned away her face. Helen ran her fingers through her unruly hair, and looked down helplessly at the girl huddled before her in terror. She reached down, and taking her under the arms lifted her to her feet.

—Julie, what is the matter with you?

—Has he gone?

—What? Are you hurt? Take your hands away and let me look at you. You haven't taken anything, have you?

Julie, her fingers pressing her eyes, began to moan. Helen pulled open the door of the cabinet above the handbasin and checked swiftly through the bottles there. She said in exasperation:

—This will have to stop, Julie. You're behaving like a child. You are looking for attention. Are you listening to me?

But Julie went on moaning. She sat on the edge of the bath now, her shoulders trembling. Helen threw up her hands and groaned at the ceiling.

—You're impossible, she cried, and left the room. Down the stairs Julie's cries followed her.

—You hate me! You hate me! You want to see me dead!

Helen went to the window and with trembling fingers lit a cheroot. This would have to stop.

She crushed out the cheroot with a savage twist of her fingers and went into the empty room where their cases were stored. Gasping with the effort she hauled them out and piled them on the couch. Julie came down the stairs, and Helen worked steadily on, pretending not to notice her.

—Don't leave me, Helen, she said mournfully.

Helen paused, but did not turn. She said:

—We have to leave today, Julie.

—I know.

—And then you're going away. You decided, didn't you?

—*You* decided. *You* did. I decided nothing. It was you!

Helen beat her fists on the battered case before her, then ran a hand over her forehead, her mouth.

—O Julie Julie Julie.

She turned, and they looked at each other. Julie lowered her eyes and pulled in the corners of her mouth. She touched the cases piled before her, her face betraying an ill-controlled, frantic incomprehension of these square, heavy things. Helen said gently:

—We're leaving today, Julie. You haven't forgotten. It's what you want. You want to leave here, don't you? The summer is over.

Julie nodded dumbly, and stepped back from the couch. She lifted her hands and opened her mouth to speak, then turned away in silence. As she went to the door Helen watched her, and shook her head.

Julie stood in the doorway and looked out across the sound. The brittle autumn sunlight danced on the water and the far islands seemed to shift and tremble in their distance. Helen came behind her and touched the down on her neck. Julie started, and as though the touch had sprung some hidden switch she began to speak tonelessly.

—I want to get married. I want to have a baby.

—Of course you do.

—My mother worries about me. She asks what are my plans. What can I tell her? And I'm weak. I feel sorry for her. I want to tell her I've found someone. That everything is all right. That everything is . . . all right.

She sighed, and turned back to the room. With her hands against the door frame she halted. Helen spoke to her, but she was not listening. A bird called to her across the reaches of the sea. Helen took Julie's face in her hands, and covered her ears with her palms, and in this new silence Julie seemed to hear vaguely someone screaming, a ghost voice familiar yet distant, as though it were coming from beyond the frontiers of sleep.

NIGHTWIND

He shuffled down the corridor, trying the handles of the blind white doors. From one room there came sounds, a cry, a soft phrase of laughter, and in the silence they seemed a glimpse of the closed, secret worlds he would never enter. He leaned against the wall and held his face in his hands. There were revels below, savage music and the clatter of glasses, and outside in the night a wild wind was blowing.

Two figures came up from the stairs and started toward him. One went unsteadily on long, elegantly tailored legs, giggling helplessly. The other leaned on his supporting elbow a pale tapering arm, one hand pressed to her bare collarbone.

—Why Morris, what is it?

They stood and gazed at him foolishly, ripples of laughter still twitching their mouths. He pushed himself away from the wall, and hitched up his trousers. He said:

—'S nothing. Too much drink. That you David?

The woman took a tiny step away from them and began to pick at her disintegrating hairdo. David licked the point of his upper lip and said:

—Listen Mor, are you all right? Mor.

—Looking for my wife, said Mor.

Suddenly the woman gave a squeal of laughter, and the two men turned to look at her.

—I thought of something funny, she said simply, and covered her mouth. Mor stared at her, his eyebrows moving. He grinned and said:

—I thought you were Liza.

The woman snickered, and David whispered in his ear:

—That's not Liza. That's . . . what is your name anyway?

—Jean, she said, and glared at him. He giggled and took her by the arm.

—Jean, I want you to meet Mor. You should know your host, after all.

The woman said:

—I wouldn't be a Liza if you paid me.

—Mother of God, said Mor, a bubble bursting on his lips.

David frowned at her for shame and said:

—You must be nice to Mor. He's famous.

—Never heard of him.

—You see, Mor? She never heard of you. Your own guest and she never heard of you. What do you think of that?

—Balls, said Mor.

—O now. Why are you angry? Is it because of what they are all saying? Nobody listens to that kind of talk. You know that. We're all friends here, aren't we, Liza—

—Jean.

—And this is a grand party you're throwing here, Mor, but no one listens to talk. We know your success is nothing to do with . . . matrimonial graft.

On the last words the corner of David's mouth moved as a tight nerve uncoiled. Mor looked at him with weary eyes, then walked away from them and turned down the stairs. David called after him:

—Where are you going, man?

But Mor was gone.

—Well, said the woman. Poor Mor is turning into quite a wreck. These days he even has to pretend he's drunk.

David said nothing, but stared at the spot where Mor had disappeared. The woman laughed, and taking his arm she pressed it against her side and said:

—Let's go somewhere quiet.

—Shut your mouth, David told her.

Downstairs Mor wandered through the rooms. The party was ending, and most of the guests had left. In the hall a tiny fat man leaned against the wall, his mouth open and his eyes closed. A tall girl with large teeth, his daughter, was punching his shoulder and yelling something in his ear. She turned to Mor for help, and he patted her arm absently and went on into the drawing room. There in the soft light a couple were dancing slowly, while others sat about in silence, looking at their hands. In the corner a woman in a white dress stood alone, a little uncertain, clutching an empty glass. She watched his unsteady progress toward her.

—There you are, he said, and grinning he touched the frail white stuff of her gown. She said nothing, and he sighed.

—All right, Liza, so I'm drunk. So what?

—So nothing. I said nothing. Your tie is crooked.

His hands went to the limp black bow at his neck, and went away again.

—It's coming apart, he said. The knot is coming apart.

—Yes.

He held her eyes for a moment, and looked away. He said:

—You have a sobering effect, Liza. How do you live with yourself?

—You always pretend to be drunker than you are and then you blame me. That's all.

—You know, I met a woman upstairs and thought it was you. She was laughing and I thought it was you. Imagine.

He put his hands into the pockets of his jacket and looked at the room. The couple had stopped dancing, and were standing motionless now in the middle of the floor, their arms around each other as though they had forgotten to disentangle them. Mor said:

—What are they waiting for? Why don't they go home?

—You hate them, Liza said. Don't you?

—Who?

—All of them. All these people—our friends.

He looked at her, his eyebrows lifted.

—No. I'm sorry for them—for us. Look at it. The new Ireland. Sitting around at the end of a party wondering why we're not happy. Trying to find what it is we've lost.

—O Mor, don't start all that.

He smiled at her, and murmured:

—No.

David put his head around the door, and when he saw them he smiled and shot at them with a finger and thumb. He crossed the room with exaggerated stealth, looking over his shoulder at imaginary pursuers. He stopped near them and asked from the corner of his mouth:

—They get him yet?

—Who? said Liza, smiling at his performance.

Mor frowned at him, and shook his head, but David pretended not to notice.

—Why, your murderer, of course.

Liza's mouth fell open, the glass shook in her hand, and then was still. David went on:

—You mean you didn't know about it? O come on now, Liza, I thought you and Mor had arranged it. You know—we've got everything at our party including a murderer loose in the grounds with the cops chasing him. You didn't know, Liza?

—Shut up, David.

—O excuse me, said David, grinning, and coughed behind his hand. Liza turned to him.

—David, what is this joke all about? Seriously now.

—Well Liz, it's no joke. Some tinker stabbed his girlfriend six times in the heart tonight. The guards had him cornered here when the rain came on. The way I heard it they left some green recruit to watch for him while they all trooped back to Celbridge for their raincoats. Anyway, they say he's somewhere in the grounds, but knowing the boys he's probably in England by now. Come over to the window and you can see the lights. It's all very exciting.

Liza took a drink and laid down her glass. She said quietly, without raising her head:

—Why didn't you tell me, Mor?

—I forgot.

—You forgot.

—Yes. I forgot.

David looked from one of them to the other, grinning sardonically. He said:

—Perhaps, Liza, he didn't want to frighten you?

Mor turned and looked at David, his lips a thin pale line.

—You have a loud mouth, David.

He moved away from them, then paused and said:

—And uncurl your lip when you talk to me. Or I might be tempted to wipe that sneer off your face.

The smile faded, and David said coldly:

—No offence meant, Mor.

—And none taken.

—Then why are you so angry?

Mor laughed, a short, cold sound.

—I haven't been angry in years.

He stalked away, and in silence they watched him go. Then Liza laughed nervously and said:

—Take no notice of him, David. He's a bit drunk. You know.

David shrugged his shoulders and smiled at her.

—I must go home.

In the hall Liza helped him into his coat. He said lightly:

—Why don't you come over to the house and visit me some day? The old bachelor life gets very dreary.

She glanced at him with a small sly smile.

—For what? she asked.

He pursed his lips and turned to the door. With his hand on the lock he said stiffly:

—I'm . . . I'm very fond of you, Liza.

She laughed, and looked down at her dress in confusion.

—Of me? O you're not.

—I am, Liza.

—You shouldn't say things like that. Good night, David.

But neither moved. They stood and gazed at each other, and Liza's breath quickened. She moved swiftly to the door and pulled it open, and a blast of wind came in to disturb the hall. She stepped out on the porch with him. The oaks were lashing their branches together, and they had voices that cried and groaned. Black rain was falling, and in the light from the door the lawn was a dark, ugly sea. She opened her mouth to speak, closed it, then turned away from him and said:

—Call me.

She stood very still and looked out at the darkness, and the damp wind lifted her hair. David moved to touch her, and dropped his hand. He said:

—I'll call you tomorrow.

—No. Not tomorrow.

—When?

—I must go, David.

With her head bent she turned and hurried back along the hall.

All the guests had left the drawing room, and Mor sat alone in a high, winged chair, a glass in his hand and a bottle beside him on a low table. His tie had at last come undone, and his eyes were faintly glazed. Liza went to the couch and straightened a cushion. From the floor she gathered up a cigarette end and an overturned glass. He watched her, his chin on his breast. He said thickly:

—What's wrong with you?

—Nothing. Have they all gone?

—I suppose so.

She went to the tall window beside his chair and drew back the curtains. The wind pounded the side of the house, and between gusts the rain whispered softly on the glass. Down past the black, invisible fields, little lights were moving. She said:

—I wonder why he killed her.

—They say he wanted to marry her and she wouldn't have him. I think she was maybe a man-eater. A tart. He killed her. Happens every day, these days.

There was silence but for the wind and rain beating, and the faint sighing of the trees. Mor said:

—I suppose David made his usual pass?

She moved her shoulders, and he grinned up at her, showing his teeth. She said:

—He asked if . . . he asked me to go with him. Tonight. He asked would I go with him.

—Did he, now? And why didn't you?

She did not answer. He poured himself another drink.

—I know how David's mind works, he said. He thinks I don't deserve you. He's wrong, though—God help me.

—You have a nasty mind.

—Yes. Though he must have been encouraged when I took the job. That sent me down a little farther.

He looked at her where she stood in the shadows watching the night. He frowned and asked:

—Do you despise me too?

—For taking the job? Why should I? Are you ashamed?

—No, no. Your father is very good to do so much for me. Yes, I'm ashamed.

—Why?

—Don't act, Liza.

—It was your decision. If you had kept on writing I would have stood by you. We would have managed. Daddy could have—

She bit her lip, and Mor laughed.

—Go on, he said. Daddy could have kept us. You're right. Kind, generous daddy would have come along with his money-bags to sour our lives. Where's the use in talking. Me a writer? I'd be laughed out of the county. The bar in the Grosvenor Arms would collapse after a week of the laughing. Did you hear how mad Mor knocked up old man Fitz's daughter and moved into the big house and now says he's writing a book? Did you ever hear the likes? No, Liza. This place produced me and will destroy me if I try to break free. All this crowd understands is the price of a heifer and the size of the new car and the holiday in Spain and those godblasted dogs howling for blood. No.

She said quietly:

—If you hated these people so much, why did you marry into them?

—Because, Liza my dear, I didn't know I was marrying into them.

There was a long silence, then Liza spoke:

—It wasn't my fault he died, she said, sadly defiant.

Mor turned away from her in the chair and threw up his hands.

—Always, he said. Always it comes to your mind. Blaming me.

She did not speak, and he leaned toward her, whispering:

—Blaming me.

She joined her hands before her and sighed, holding her eyes fixed on the dark gleam of the glass before her. He said:

—Well why don't you just trot along now after old David there. Sure maybe he can give you a better one. One that will live longer and make you happy.

She swung about to face him. Her eyes blazed, and she said:

—All right then, Mor, if you want a fight you'll get one.

For a moment they stared at each other, and her anger went away. She turned back to the window.

—Well? Mor asked, and the word rang in the silence. She lifted her shoulders slowly, allowed them to fall. Mor nodded.

—Yes, he said. We've had it all before.

He stood up unsteadily, pressing his fingers on the arm of the chair for support. He went and stood beside her at the window. She said:

—They're still searching. Look at the lights.

Side by side they stood and watched the tiny flashes move here and there in the dark. Suddenly she said:

—If he got to the stables he could come in through the side door. If he did I'd hide him.

He stared at her, and feeling his eyes on her she set her mouth firmly and said:

—I would, I'd hide him. And then in the morning I'd get him out and bring him to Dublin and put him on the boat for England, for Liverpool or some place.

She reached out blindly and took his hand. There were tears on her face, they fell, each gathering to itself a little light and flashing in the darkness of the window.

—We could do that if he came, couldn't we, Mor? It wouldn't be a bad thing to do. It wouldn't be a crime, I mean, would it? Out there in the dark with the rain and everything and thinking about all the things—thinking and thinking. It wouldn't be wrong to help him, Mor?

He took her in his arms and held her head on his shoulder. She was trembling.

—No, he said softly. It wouldn't be a bad thing.

She began to sob quietly, and he lifted her head and smiled at her.

—Don't cry, Liza. There now.

The door-bell rang, and her eyes filled with apprehension. Without a word she moved past him and left the room.

Mor stood and looked about him. Long ago when he first saw this room he had thought it beautiful, and now it was one of the few things left which had not faded. The shaded lamps took from the warm walls of lilac a soft, full light, it touched everything, the chairs, the worn carpet, with gentle fingers. On the table beside him a half-eaten sandwich lay beside his bottle. There was an olive transfixed on a wooden pin. Muted voices came in from the hall, and outside in the fields a shout flared like a flame in the dark and then was blown away. Mor lifted his glass, and when the amber liquid moved, all the soft light of the room seemed to shift with it. He felt something touch him. It was as though all the things he had ever lost had now come back to press upon his heart with a vast sadness. He stared at the table, at the little objects, the bread and the bottle, the olive dead on its pin.

Liza came back, her hands joined before her, and the knuckles white. She stopped in the middle of the room and looked blankly about her, as if she were dazed.

—What is it? he asked. Who was at the door?

—A guard.

—What did he want?

—What?

—What did he want? The guard.

—O, the guard. He wanted to use the 'phone.

She looked at him, and blinked rapidly twice.

—They found him, she said. He hanged himself in the long meadow.

She examined the room once again with vague eyes, then she sighed, and went away. He sat down to finish his drink, and after a time went out and climbed the stairs.

Liza was lying in bed, the lamp beside her throwing a cruel light over her drawn face. He sat beside her and watched her. Her eyes were open, staring up into the dimness. In the silence there was the sound of the rain against the window. She said, so softly he barely heard her:

—We missed so much.

He leaned down and kissed her forehead. She did not move. He put his hand over her breast, feeling the nipple cold and small through the silk of her nightgown.

—Liza.

She turned away from him, and when she spoke her voice was muffled by the sheets.

—Bring me a glass of water, Morris. My mouth is dry.

He moved away from her, and switched off the light. He went down the stairs in the darkness, the air cold and stale against his face. On quiet feet he returned to the drawing room and poured another, last drink. Then he went and stood at the dark window, and listened to the wind blowing in the trees.

SUMMER VOICES

. . . Shalt thou hope. His truth shall compass thee with a shield. Thou shalt not be afraid of the terror of the night, of the arrow that flies in the day, of the business that walks in the dark, of invasion or of the noonday devil.

The old voice droned on, and the boy wondered at the words. He looked through the window at the countryside, the fields floating in the summer heat. On Hallowe'en people must stay indoors for fear of the devils that fly in the darkness. Once he had heard them crying, those dark spirits, and she said it was only the wind. But to think of the wind in the black trees out on the marsh was almost as bad as imagining devils. And late that night from the window of his bedroom he saw huge shadows of leaves dancing on the side of the house, and the circle of light from the street lamp shivering where it fell on the road.

—Are you going to ask her?

—What?

The little girl frowned at him and leaned close to his ear, her curls falling about her face. She whispered:

—Ssh, will you. Are you going to ask her can we go? He said seven days and the tide will be up in an hour. Go on and ask her.

He nodded.

—In a minute.

She stuck out her tongue at him. Through his crossed legs he touched his fists on the cool tiles of the floor. The old woman in the chair before him licked her thumb and turned a page of the black missal. The thin paper crackled and the ribbons stirred where they hung from the torn spine.

—I will deliver him and glorify him. I will fill him with length of days and I will show him my salvation.

She raised her eyes from the page and glared at them over the metal rims of her spectacles. Crossly she said:

—What are you two whispering about there?

—Tantey, can we go for a swim? the little girl cried and jumped to her feet. The old woman smiled and shook her head.

—O it's a swim is it? You'd rather be off swimming now than listening to the words of God.

—Ah but it's a lovely day, Tantey. Can we go, can we?

—I suppose so. But mind now and be careful. And you're not to stay out late.

She closed the missal and kissed reverently the tattered binding. Groaning she pulled herself up from her chair and hobbled to the door. There she paused and turned, and said to the boy who still sat on the floor with his legs crossed:

—Mind what I say now. Be back here early.

When she was gone the girl went and sat in the armchair, and with her shoulders bent she mimicked the old woman, intoning:

—Achone achone the Lord and all his angels are coming to damn us all to hell.

—Ah stop that, said the boy.

—Nor you needn't be afeared of the devil in the day. Achone achone O.

—I told you to stop it.

—All right. All right. Don't be always bossing me around.

She made a face at him and tramped from the room, saying over her shoulder:

—I'm going to get the bikes and if you're not out before I count ten I'm going on my own.

The boy did not move. Sunlight fell through the tiny window above the stove. The radiance of the summer afternoon wove shadows about him. Beyond the window a dead tree stood like a crazy old naked man, a blackbird hopping among its twisted branches. The boy stood up and went into what had once been the farmyard—the barn and the sties had long since crumbled. After the dimness of the kitchen the light here burned his eyes. He moved across to stand under the elm tree and listen to the leaves. Out over the green fields the heat lay heavy, pale blue and shimmering. In the sky a bird circled slowly. He lifted his head and gazed into the thickness of the leaves. Light glinted gold through the branches. He stood motionless, his arms hanging at his sides, listening, and slowly, from the far fields, the strange cry floated to his ears, a needle of sound that pierced the stillness. He held his breath. The voice hung poised a moment in the upper airs, a single liquid note, then slowly faded back into the fields, and died away, leaving the silence deeper than before.

—Are you coming or are you just going to stand there all day?

He turned. The girl stood between the two ancient bicycles, a saddle held in each of her small hands.

—I'm coming, he grunted.

They mounted and rode slowly down to the gate, where he halted while the girl swung carelessly out into the road. When he was sure of safety he pedalled furiously after her.

—You'll get killed some day, he said when he was beside her again.

The girl turned up her nose and shook her hair in the warm wind.

—You're an awful scaredy cat, she said contemptuously.

—I just don't want to get run over, that's all.

—Hah.

She trod on the pedals and glided away from him. He watched her as she sailed along, her bony knees rising and falling. She took her hands from the handlebars and waved them in the air.

—You'll fall off, he shouted.

She glanced over her shoulder at him and pulled her hair above her head, and the long gold tresses coiled about her pale arms. Her teeth glinted as she laughed.

Free now they slowed their pace and leisurely sailed over the road, tyres whispering in the soft tar. The fields trembled on either side of them. Sometimes the girl sang in her high-pitched, shaky voice, and the notes carried back to him, strangely muted by the wide fields, a distant, piping song. Tall shoots of vicious grass waving from the ditches scratched their legs. The boy watched the land as it moved slowly past him, the sweltering meadows, the motionless trees, and high up on the hill the cool deep shadows under Wild Wood.

—Listen, the girl said, allowing him to overtake her. Do you think they'll let us see him?

—I don't know.

—Jimmy would. He'd let me see him all right. But there's bound to be others.

She brooded, gazing at her feet circling under her.

—How do you know they'll find him? the boy asked.

—Jimmy said so.

—Jimmy.

—You shut up. You don't know anything about him.

—He's dirty, the boy said sullenly.

—You never saw him.

—I did.

—Well he's not dirty. And anyway I don't care. I'm in love with him, so there.

—He's dirty and he's old and he's mad, too.

—I don't care. I love him. I'd love him to kiss me.

She closed her eyes and puckered her lips at the sky. Suddenly she turned and pushed the boy violently, so that he almost lost his balance. She watched him try to control the wobbling wheels, and she screamed with laughter. Then she sailed ahead of him once again, crying:

—You're only jealous, you are.

The girl disappeared around a bend in the road, and he stepped down from the machine. He plodded scowling up the first steep slope of Slane Hill.

When he came round the bend he found the girl standing beside her bicycle waiting for him, her hands at her mouth.

—Listen, she said, and grasped his arm. There's somebody up there.

At the top of the hill a dark figure was huddled in the ditch at the side of the road.

—It's only a man, the boy said.

—I don't like the look of him.

—You're afraid.

—I am not. I just don't like the look of him.

—Not so brave now, the boy sneered.

—All right then, smartie. Come on.

They began the climb. Sweat gathered at the corners of their eyes and on their lips. Under their hands the rubber of the grips on the handlebars grew moist and sticky. Flies came and buzzed about them. They lowered their heads and pushed the awkward black machines to the crest of the hill. Below them now was the sea, warm and blue and glittering with flakes of silver light. A cool breeze came up over the sandy fields, carrying a faint bitterness of salt against their mouths. A stirring beside them in the ditch. A hoarse voice. Panic stabbed them. They leaped into the saddles and careered off down the hill, while behind them a ragged, strangely uncertain figure stood dark against the sky, querulously calling.

The air whistled by their ears as they raced along the pitted road. The sea was coming to meet them, the dunes rose up green and gold, sea salt cutting their nostrils, the sun whirling like a rimless spoked wheel of gold, sea and dunes rushing, then abruptly the road ended, their tyres sank in the sand and they toppled from the saddles.

For a while they lay panting, and listened to the sea whispering gently on the shore. Then the girl raised her head and looked back up the hill.

—He's gone, she whispered hoarsely.

The boy sat up and rubbed his knee.

—I hurt myself.

—I said he's gone.

—Who is?

—The fellow up on the hill. He's gone.

The boy shaded his eyes and gazed back along the road. He pursed his lips and murmured vaguely:

—O yes.

She caught his wrist in her bony fingers.

—Did you hear what he was shouting? Did you hear what he called you?

—Me?

—He was shouting at you. He called you mister.

—Did he?

—Didn't you hear him?

He did not answer, but stood up and brushed the sand from his faded cord trousers.

—Come on, he said, and grasping her hand he pulled her to her feet. The tide is up. We'll leave the bikes here.

He walked away from her, limping slightly. She stared after him for a moment and then began to follow. She scowled at his back and cried:

—You're a right fool!

—Come on.

Through a gap in the dunes they passed down to the beach. The sea was quiet, a bowl of calm blue waters held in the arms of the horseshoe bay. Lines of sea-wrack scored the beach, evidence of the changing limits of the tide. They walked slowly toward the pier, a grey finger of stone accusing the ocean.

—I'd love a swim, the little girl said.

—Why didn't you bring your togs?

—I think I'll go in in my skin.

—You will not.

—If I met some fellow swimming underwater wouldn't he get a great shock?

Giggling she tucked the hem of her dress into her knickers and waded into the sea. She splashed about, drenching herself. Her cries winged out over the water like small swift birds. The boy watched her, then he turned away and moved on again.

—Wait for me, she cried, and came thrashing out of the sea.

At the end of the pier a bent old man was sitting on a bollard, his back turned toward them. The girl ran ahead and began to dance excitedly around him. The boy came up and stopped behind the old man. He put his hands into his pockets and stared out to sea with studied indifference, softly whistling. A distant sail trembled on the horizon.

—And did your auntie let you go? the old man was asking of the girl, mocking her. He had a low, hoarse voice, and he spoke slowly, as though to hide an impediment.

—She did, the girl said, and laughed slyly. It was such a grand day.

—Aye, it's a great day.

He turned his head and considered the boy a moment.

—And who's this young fellow?

—That's my brother.

—Aye now? he said blankly.

He turned back to the sea, grinding his gums. The boy shifted from one foot to the other. For a while there was silence but for the faint crackling of the seaweed over on the beach. The old man spat noisily and said:

—Well, they've took him out anyway.

The girl's eyes flashed. She looked at her brother and winked.

—Did they? she said casually. Today, eh?

—Aye. Fished him out today. Didn't I tell them? Aye.

—What did they do with him, Jimmy? I suppose they took him away long ago.

—Not at all, said the old man. Sure it's no more than half an hour since he come in. Ah no. He's still down there.

He waved an arm toward the beach at his back.

—Did they just leave him there? asked the girl in surprise.

—Aye. They're gone off to get something to shift him in.

—I see.

She bit her lip, and leaned close to the old man's ear and whispered. He listened a moment, then turned and stared at her from one yellowed eye.

—What? What? You don't want to see a thing like that. Do you? What?

—We do. That's why we came. Isn't it?

She rammed her elbow into the boy's ribs.

—O yes, he said quickly. That's why we came.

The old man stared from one to the other, shook his head, then got to his feet, saying:

—Come on then, before your men come back. Begod, you're the strange ones then. Hah. Aren't you the strange ones? Heh heh.

They walked back along the pier, the girl rushing excitedly between the old man and the boy, urging them to hurry. When they reached the sand the old man led them down behind the sea wall. At the edge of the waves a bundle covered in an old piece of canvas lay in the shade of the pier. The girl rushed forward and knelt beside it in the sand. The old man cried:

—Wait there now, young one. Don't touch anything there.

The three of them stood in silence and gazed down at the object where it lay in the violet shade. Out on the rocks a seabird screeched. The old man leaned down and pulled away the canvas. The boy turned away his face, but not before he had glimpsed the creature, the twisted body, the ruined face, the soft, pale swollen flesh like the flesh of a rotted fish. The girl knelt and stared, her mouth open. She whispered:

—There he is, then.

—Aye, the old man muttered. That's what the sea will do to you. The sea and the rocks. And the fish too.

The boy stood with his back to them, looking at his hands. And then a shout came from far up the beach.

—Hi! Get them children away from there! Get out of it, you old fool!

The boy looked up along the sand. Figures were running toward them, waving their fists. The old man muttered a curse and hobbled away with surprising speed over the dunes. The girl leaped to her feet and was away beside the waves, her bare feet slapping the sand and raising splashes that flashed in the sun like sparks. The boy stood motionless, and listened to her wild laughter that floated back to him on the salt air. He knelt in the sand and looked down at the strange creature lying there. He spoke a few words quietly, a message, then with care he gently replaced the canvas shroud. Then he ran away up the beach after his sister, who was already out of sight.

Some time later he found her, sitting under a thorn tree in the fields behind the beach. She was rubbing the damp sand from her feet with a handful of grass. When she saw him she sniffed derisively and said:

—O, it's you.

He lay down in the warm grass at her side, panting. Bees hummed about him.

—Did they catch you? she asked.

—No.

—That's a wonder. I thought you were going to stand there all day.

The boy said nothing, and she went on:

—Jimmy was here a minute ago. He said I was a right little bitch getting him into trouble. He's worried as anything. That fellow's not a bit mad. Anyway, he's gone now. I don't care.

She looked down at him. He was chewing a blade of grass and staring into thorns above him. She poked him with her toe.

—Are you listening to me?

—No.

He stood up, and said:

—We'll have to go home. Tantey will be worried.

—Ah, sugar on Tantey.

They found their bicycles and started home through the glimmering evening. Clouds of midges rode with them. The tiny flies found a way into their hair and under their clothes. The girl cursed them and waved her hands about her head. The boy rode on without a word, his head bent.

The old woman was indeed angry with them.

—I warned you before you went, she said, and glared at them from her chair beside the stove. I warned you. Well now you can just hop it off to bed for yourselves. Go on.

—But what about our supper, Tantey?

—You'll have no supper tonight. Get on now.

—I'm tired, anyway, the girl said carelessly when they were climbing the stairs.

By the window on the first landing the boy stopped and looked out over the countryside down to the sea. The sun was setting blood-red over the bay. He stood and watched it until it fell into the sea. When it was long gone he heard the girl's voice calling plaintively from above.

—*Where are you? Where are you?*

He climbed to her room and stood at the end of the bed, looking down at her.

—I have a pain, she said, as she twisted fitfully among the rumpled sheets, her legs thrown wide, her hand clutching her stomach. He leaned his hands on the metal bedpost and watched her. As she twisted and turned she glanced at him now and then through half-closed eyes. After a moment he looked away from her, and with his lips pursed he considered the ceiling.

—Do you want to know something? he asked.

—What? O my stomach.

—You know that fellow today? The one that shouted at us on the hill? Do you know who he was?

She was quiet now. She lay on her back and stared at him, her eyes glittering.

—No. Who was he?

—He was the other fellow. The one that got drowned. That was him.

He turned to go and she leaped forward and clutched his hand.

—Don't leave me, she begged, her eyes wide. I'm frightened. You can sleep here. Look, here, you can sleep here with me. Please.

He took his hand from hers and went to the door.

—All right, the girl cried. Go on, then. I don't want you. You didn't need to be coaxed last night. Did you, mister? Ha ha. Mister.

He left the room and closed the door quietly behind him. Strange shapes before him in the shadows of the stairs. For a while he walked about the house, treading carefully on the ancient boards. All was quiet but for the small sounds of his sister's weeping. On the top landing a black, square thing lay precariously balanced on the banister. Tantey's missal. As he passed he casually pushed it over the edge. The heavy book tumbled down the stairs, its pages fluttering.

He went into the bathroom and locked the door. On the handbasin he knelt and pushed open the small window of frosted glass set high in the wall. Darkness was approaching. Black clouds, their edges touched with red, were gathering out over the sea, and shadows were lowering on the ugly waters. A cold damp breath touched his face. In the distance a long peal of thunder rumbled. He closed the window and climbed down from the basin. He scrubbed his hands and dried them carefully, finger by finger. For a moment he was still, listening. No sounds. Then he went and stood before the mirror and gazed into it at his face for a long time.

ISLAND

He sat in the garden under the olive tree, looking past the headland toward Delos, the holy island, where it trembled on the mist. In the night the fierce wind had died, and today the sea was calm. He lit a cigarette, and the blue threads of smoke curled away into the burnished leaves above him. Cicadas sang about the scorched fields, and now and then there came the plop of a pomegranate bursting in the sun. The day would be hot.

Anna came from the cottage, a wooden tray in her hands. He watched her idly as she laid the table of rough olive wood before him, two cups, bread and white butter, grapes. She would not look at him, and her mouth was set in a tight line. From the taverna below the hill came faintly the gobbling of the turkeys. With his eyes on the road he said:

—Ever think that those birds can talk? Listen to them. *You haven't you haven't you haven't.* That's what they say.

She did not answer, and he glanced at her.

—Are you still angry? he asked.

—I'm not angry. Who said I was angry?

She hacked a lump of bread from the loaf and slapped it down on the plate. He laughed, and grinding the cigarette under his heel he said:

—You were angry last night.

—Well, that was last night.

—Don't shout.

—I'm not shouting.

She stood with her hands on her hips and glared at him, and with a shrug he turned away and looked again down the road. She said:

—Why do you sit here every morning staring like that?

—No reason.

—You're waiting for someone to come with a message or something, aren't you, so you'll have an excuse to go away and leave me.

He sighed, and rubbed his eyes. Patiently he said:

—No, Anna, I'm not waiting for anything. I just like to sit here in the morning. It's pleasant.

—While you sit here your life is going away and my life too. Why don't you write? Wasting your time like that. You're bored. You want to leave me.

—For the love of Christ, Anna.

He took her hands and pulled her down to sit in his lap. For a moment he gazed at her, watching the sun through the leaves set fire in her hair. She bit her lip, and he kissed her, pressing his mouth roughly on hers.

—Now, he said. I love you and I'm not going to leave you. Do you believe me?

She held him tightly and murmured in his ear:

—I believe you.

—Good. So let's eat.

While she poured his coffee he fingered absently the bread on his plate, tearing the soft white flesh. She watched him from the corner of her eye and said:

—We could always go on, you know.

—What?

—We could go on somewhere else. I mean if you're bored we could go, say, to Alexandria. You're always saying you'd like to go to Alexandria.

With his lips pursed he looked at her a moment, his face empty, then he turned his eyes to the road that led down to the beach and the still sea. The light was changing now as the climbing sun burned away the morning's mist, Delos was advancing and the farther islands were faintly visible. A small breeze came up from the bay and stirred the leaves of the olive tree.

—Why should I want to leave here? he murmured. It's peaceful.

She nodded sadly and took one of his cigarettes. She said:

—Why did you change so much?

—Change? Did I change?

—When we left Ireland you were full of plans and things. The first few months you were happy.

—And now?

—I don't know. You just sit around all day. You haven't worked on your book in weeks. You don't even talk anymore. Sometimes I get frightened and I think that you don't see the point of anything any longer.

She broke off and gave a small high-pitched laugh.

—Isn't that ridiculous? she said, and sat very still, watching the smoke from her cigarette, waiting. He pushed the hair away from her forehead, and she looked at him, smiling awkwardly.

—It's ridiculous, he said. I enjoy this life. You know it.

—Yes. But I mean all I meant was that maybe you're bored here and maybe we could move on somewhere else. We haven't even started to use the money from your award yet so there's no problem there. I mean I . . . Ben, I don't want to lose you, she finished weakly.

His patience at an end, he sighed and turned away from her. She looked down at the table where the shadows from the tree stirred on the wood. Soft sunlight touched the cups and plates, the bread and the small green grapes, extracting from each thing it touched a sense of the thing itself, a sense of the fragility of its existence. Then the leaves stirred, and the shadows changed, a new pattern formed, one that seemed held in place by a force from within the wood itself. Something came back to her of their life together, and she smiled. She turned to him to speak, beginning to laugh, when from behind them on the road came a voice:

—Good morning.

They turned. On the broken pillar of the gate a woman leaned, smiling at them. Neither answered her, and the woman said:

—Can you help me? I am looking for someone.

She was dressed in a black faded shirt and black trousers. Her hair, long and straight, hung down about a narrow, bony face. Her mouth was small, and painted an ugly red. The flesh of her face was burned and dry from long years under this southern sun. On the bridge of her nose a pale spot glowed where the skin was stretched tight over the bone. Her eyes were large and black.

Ben stood up uncertainly and took a step toward her, halted. He said:

—Who is it you're looking for?

The woman pushed a lank strand of hair away from her face with long, delicate fingers.

—A man, she said. He must have passed this way.

—We've seen no one. Anna spoke abruptly, and her eyes widened as though she had surprised herself. The woman glanced at her without interest and went on:

—They said in the village he came this way. Is there another road to the beach down there?

—No, Ben said. This is the only way and no one passed this morning.

The woman gazed at him, shading her eyes against the light.

—You could not miss him, she said. He is a dark man. A negro. Very tall with a red shirt open so at the neck.

Ben said nothing, and the woman's eyes grew troubled and wandered over the road down to the bay.

—I must find him, she murmured. He is . . . how would you say? His mind is gone. This morning in the village he attacked a man and almost killed him with a wine bottle. I am worried.

Ben was staring at her intently, his mouth moving. Anna stood up and went to his side. In the silence there was the sharp, clicking sound of lizards scrabbling over the rocks. From below the hill the turkeys sent up their derisive accusations. Anna's fists were clenched, and she said loudly:

—We've seen no one.

The woman turned back to them.

—You have seen no one?

—No, Anna answered her.

The woman nodded.

—Yes, she said vaguely, and then abruptly turned and started down the hill. Ben watched her go, his forehead wrinkled, and Anna pulled at his sleeve.

—Come and finish your breakfast, she said.

He did not move, and she turned away from him. On the table the wreckage of their meal lay like the dismembered parts of a complex toy.

—Will we go down for a swim? she asked, and not waiting for a reply she went into the cottage and brought out her swimsuit.

The beach was deserted. With his eyes closed he lay on the sand while she threw her awkward body about in the clear green waters. Then she came out and stood by him, tossing the water from her hair.

—I'm going to dress, she said, and went away.

After a little time he stood up and followed her into the pine grove. Here the air was cool and dim, and fragrant with the perfume of the trees. In the clearing behind the taverna he found her, standing naked with a red towel in her hands. Silver flecks of water glistened on her sun-browned skin. He stood behind a tree and watched her, pulling at his lip with a thumb and forefinger. When he stepped into the clearing she looked up quickly, and then smiled and held the towel before her.

—Go away, she said, laughing.

But without a word he caught the towel and pulled it away from her, and taking her in his arms he drew her roughly against him. She struggled, not laughing now.

—Ben, leave me alone. Ben!

She pushed him away and stepped back a pace, and he stumbled on the exposed root of a tree and fell.

—Leave me *alone,* Ben.

She stood there against the trees, breathing heavily, her eyes flashing. With her mouth open to speak she suddenly stiffened, and stared past him. He turned quickly, lifting himself on his hands, in time to glimpse something flitting through the trees, a dark figure moving swiftly, silently away. He slowly turned his head and grinned at her. From far off in the trees came the sound of someone calling once, and then silence. Anna stood very still, watching him, then she quickly pulled on her clothes and went past him where he lay watching her with cold amusement.

He followed her at a distance up the hill. When he reached the garden he stopped to look back down to the beach, the flashing sea. Then he went into the cottage.

The shutters were drawn against the fierce light, and she sat on the bed among shadows, her head bent, gazing into her cupped hands as if she held there some small part of a great desolation. He sat beside her, and she fell against him, her arms about his neck.

—There now, he said, and patted her shoulder.

They lay now together on the bed, and he lit a cigarette. She said:

—Why does everything have to end?

—What are you talking about?

—You're going to leave me. I know it.

She lifted her head to look at him, but he said nothing, and would not meet her eyes. She lay down again, sighing.

—What will I do? she asked helplessly. What will I do? I used to be happy. Being happy is all I'm good for.

Suddenly she punched his shoulder hard, and buried her face in the pillow.

—Why are you doing this to me? she cried. Why?

—I don't know.

He looked up into the shadows, at the smoke from his cigarette twisting in blue wreaths. Through a chink in the shutters a gold sword of light pierced the shadows and embedded itself in the floor beside him.

—You can only dance as long as the music lasts, he said.

—You and your music. I'll never forgive you, Ben. Not ever. You have ruined me.

—No I haven't. One tune is ended. Something stopped it.

—Which is a fancy way of saying you're fed up. You always call a spade a shovel. I hate you.

For a time they were quiet, then she raised herself on her elbows and said:

—I should have known before we started. I should have known. Because I'm too . . . too . . .

She paused, searching for the word.

—I'm too innocent for you. Too easy to understand. I've never killed anyone.

He turned his head and stared at her, and she looked away from him and bit her knuckles. Shadows stirred about them, strange shapes moved silently around the bed. After a long time she whispered:

—I'm afraid, Ben.

—Yes.

The cicadas sang about the scorched fields, through the shutters they could hear the brittle music. Outside the day trembled with white heat, but the sun had fallen past its highest point, and the afternoon was beginning its slow descent.

DE RERUM NATURA

The old man was hosing the garden when the acrobats appeared. They were unexpected, to say the least. Elves, now, would not have surprised him, or goblins. But acrobats! Still, he got used to them, and in the last weeks came to value them above all else the world could offer. Glorious weeks, the best of the year, sweltering dog days drenched with sun and the singing of skylarks. He spent them in the garden, thrashing about in the waist-high grass, delirious with the heat and a suffocating sense of the countless lives throbbing all around him, the swarming ants, the birds in the trees, glittering bright blue flies, the lizards and spiders, his beloved bees, not to mention the things called inanimate, the earth itself, all these, breeding and bursting and killing. Sometimes it all became too much, and then he would take the hose and saturate the garden, howling in a rapture of mad glee and disgust. It was at the end of one of these galas that he first saw the acrobats.

George and Lucy hardly recognised him. If they had met him in the garden they might have taken him for a tree, burned mahogany as he was, with that long beard like grizzled ivy. He had stopped using the cutthroat for fear that it would live up to its name some morning, and he had no intention of giving them by accident an excuse for an orgy of mourning. Anyway, at that time it looked as if he would soon starve to death. Then he discovered that the garden was rich with food, cabbages and rhubarb, potatoes, raspberries, all manner of things flourishing under the weeds. There were even roses, heavy bloodred blooms, unsettling. His fits of fury with the hose helped all this growth. What a silence there was after the deluge, and in the silence the stealthy drip of water slipping from leaf to limb to root, into the parched earth.

The acrobats appeared through a mist of sparkling light, a troupe of short stout fellows in black striped leotards, with furred bandy legs and leather straps on their arms and incongruously dainty black dancing pumps. An hallucination, he said, sure that in a moment they would vanish, leaving nothing behind but a faintly reverberating *ping*! But he was wrong. They set up their trampoline and parallel bars in the clearing at the bottom of the orchard and began to leap and prance about, clapping their hands and urging each other on with enthusiastic squeaks and cries. Allez up! There was one woman only, fat, with hot dark eyes, who managed to be the undisputed centre of the show even though she did nothing more than pose, and toss her hair, and flash those brimming eyes. The first performance was brief, and they went away puffing and sweating.

Next day they were back. He was tending the hives when he saw through the trees a figure sailing up and down with leisurely grace on the trampoline. Already he detected a distinct improvement in their act. They rounded it off with a human pyramid, a wobbly edifice fraught with unacknowledged hilarity. He sat in the shade of an apple tree and watched them bouncing and tumbling, wondering if he was expected to applaud. To the third show he brought along a saucepan and a pair of forks, with which he produced a tattoo as of a snare drum during those moments of stillness and suspense before the last daring splendour of a stunt was attempted. The woman waddled forward, smiling haughtily, and swept him a low bow.

He poured rapturous accounts of their antics into crazed messianic letters which he stuffed stampless in the postbox in the village at dead of night, laughing in the dark at the thought of the storm and panic they would precipitate on the breakfast tables of his family and friends. No replies came, which surprised and annoyed him, until he realised that all to whom he had written were dead, save his son and daughter-in-law, who arrived in the heart of the country one burning noon and laid siege to his sanctuary.

—He must be really bad this time, said George.

—No stamp, said Lucy. Typical.

The house was silent, the windows blind, the doors barricaded against them. They hammered on it with their fists, and heard within the sound of muffled laughter. They called to him, pleaded, and were turning away when suddenly there erupted a plangent discord of piano music, followed by a shriek of castors rolling on stone. The door collapsed slowly into the hall, and there was the old man grinning at them from behind the piano, his little blue eyes glinting in the gloom. His clothes were in tatters, his feet bare and crusted with grime. He looked more than anything like a baby, the bald dome and bandy legs, the eyes, the gums, an ancient mischievous baby.

—My god, Lucy murmured, appalled.

—That's right! that's me! the old man cried. He executed a brief dance on the flagstones, capering and gesticulating, then stopped and glared at them.

—What do you want?

George stepped forward, stumbled over the fallen door, and blushed.

—Hello there! he yelled. How are you . . . ?

The heartiness fell sickeningly flat, and he blanched. Although well into middle age, George had the air of a gawky, overgrown schoolboy. His long thin frame gave an impression first of all of paleness, pale eyes and hands, pale dusty hair. When he smiled, the tip of a startlingly red tongue appeared between his teeth. There was an eggstain like a bilious sunburst on his tie. The old man eyed him unenthusiastically and said with heavy sarcasm:

—Rakish as ever, eh Georgie? Well come on, get in here, get in.

Lucy did not stir, rooted by her fury to the spot. How dare this decrepit madman order her George about! A hot flush blossomed on her forehead. The old man smiled at her mockingly, and led his son away down the hall.

He conducted them on a tour of his kingdom as though they were strangers. The house was a shambles. There were pigeons in the bedrooms, rats in the kitchen. That was fine with him, he said. Life everywhere. He told them how he locked himself out one day and broke the door off its hinges to get in again, then had to jam the piano against it to hold it up. The old woman from the farms in the hills who took care of him fled after that episode. He lived in the drawing-room, in a lair of old blankets and newspapers and cobwebs, yet he felt that his presence penetrated every nook and corner of the house like a sustained note of music. Even the mice in the attic were aware of him, he knew it.

In a corridor upstairs Lucy grabbed her husband's arm and whispered fiercely:

—How long are we going to stay fooling around here?

George ducked his head as though avoiding a blow. He glanced nervously at the old man shambling ahead of them and muttered:

—It's all right now, don't fuss, we've plenty of time.

Lucy sighed wearily, and closed her eyes. She was a plump woman, still pretty, with large expressive breasts which trembled when she was angry. There was a damp sheen on her nose and chin, and she exuded a faint whiff of sweat. Summer did not agree with her.

—Tell him we're taking him away, she said. Tell him about the home.

—Lucy, he's my *father.*

He turned his face resolutely away from her and quickened his step. Once again he noticed how odd this house was, with its turrets and towers and pink and white timbering, like an enormous birthday cake set down in the midst of the fields. Only his father had felt at home here, while the rest of the family dreamt vague fitful dreams of escape into a world free of his malevolent, insidious gaiety. George remembered, with a shudder, his childhood, the genteel penury, the mockery of the village, the friends in whose homes he sat with his hands pressed between his bony knees, inwardly wailing in envy of the simple, dull normalcy of lives where fathers in suits and ties returned at evening, scowling and tired, to newspapers and slippers and huge fried teas. A door at the end of a corridor led into one of the turrets, a tiny eyrie of glass and white wood, capped by an unexpectedly graceful little spire. Here, suspended and insulated in this bubble of light, the old man had spent his days working out with meticulous logic the details of his crazy schemes, oblivious of his wife's slow dying, the children's despair. George felt stirring within him the first tendrils of confused rage, and he retreated into the corridor. His father came trotting after him.

—Wait there, I want to show you my plans for the distillery.

George halted.

—Distillery . . . ?

—Aye. With potatoes. The place is full of them out there.

Lucy, behind them, let fall a shrill gulp of laughter.

They had lunch in the ruined dining-room, raw carrots, beans, mounds of raspberries, honey. Lucy found knives and forks and three cracked plates, but the old man would have none of these niceties.

—Do animals use forks? he asked, leaning across the table, his eyes wide. He had put in his dentures. They lent his face an odd look, both comical and savage.

—Well, do they?

—We're not animals, she said sullenly.

He grinned. That was the answer he had wanted.

—O yes we are, my girl, yes we are, poor forked animals.

Lucy's chest began to surge, and her forehead darkened, and George, his legs twisted under the table in a knot of anxiety, searched frantically for a way to head off the argument he could see approaching.

—Well listen, why, why don't you tell us about these fellows in the garden that you see, these acrobats?

The old man's eyes grew shifty, and he munched on a carrot and mumbled to himself. Then he sat upright suddenly.

—They dance, you know. They have this little dance when they're flying in that tells the ones coming out where the source is, how far, what direction, precisely. You don't believe me? I'll show you. O aye, they dance all right.

Lucy looked blankly from the old man to George and back again, and in her bafflement forgot herself and ate a handful of beans off the bare boards.

—Who? she asked.

The old man glared.

—Who what? Bees, of course. Haven't I just told you? Snails too.

—Snails! George cried, trying desperately to sound astounded and intrigued, and fired off a nervous laugh like a rapid volley of hiccups.

—*Yuck,* Lucy grunted softly in disgust.

The old man was offended.

—What's wrong? Snails, what's wrong with snails? They dance. Everything dances.

He picked up the honeycomb. The thick amber syrup dripped unnoticed into his lap. His lips moved mutely for a moment, striving painfully to find the words. Grime gathered at the corners of his mouth.

—It takes six hundred bees to gather a pound of honey. Six hundred, you'll say, that's not bad, but do you know how much flying it takes? Twenty-five thousand miles. Did you know that, did you?

They shook their heads slowly, gazing at him with open mouths. He was trembling, and all at once tears started from his eyes.

—Think of all that work, thousands of miles, on the flowers, that labour, the queen getting fat, the eggs hatching, then the frost, thousands dead, another world. Another world! You'll say it's blind instinct, cruel, like a machine, nature's slaves, and you're right, you're right, but listen to me, what is it at the centre, how do they keep it all going? *They dance.*

Suddenly he leaped from his chair and began to zoom about the room, bowing and gliding, crooning and laughing, the tears flowing, waving the comb aloft and scattering honey on the chairs, the table, until at last he tripped on the fender and fell into the fireplace in a storm of dust and soot and cobwebs, out of which his voice rose like the tolling of a bell.

—Poor forked animals, and they dance.

Days passed. Lucy and George cleared the spiders and the mousedirt out of the big front bedroom, and there they spent the hot nights, waking up at all hours to engage in one-sided arguments. George dithered, lapsed into a kind of moral catatonia, smiled a chilling smile, giggled sometimes inexplicably. Once he interrupted her in full flight by saying dreamily:

—Did you know that whales sing? O yes, in the depths of the oceans, songs. So he says.

—George! Get a grip of yourself.

—Yes, yes. But still . . .

After the first day the old man ceased to acknowledge their presence, and went back to his life in the garden. Often they saw the water cascading in the orchard, and heard his howls. When he met them in the house he would glance at them furtively and smile to himself, like a man recognising familiar, harmless phantoms. Lucy's rage turned into despair. She confronted her husband with final, unavoidable decisions, which somehow he always managed to avoid. The weather held, sun all day, breathless nights. She became obsessed with herself, her sweat, damp hair, scalding flesh. The taps in the bathroom did not work. She smelled, she was sure of it. This could not go on.

—George, it's him or me, I mean it, make your choice.

His head sank between his shoulders, and he cracked his knuckles. That noise made her want to scream. He said:

—What do you mean, you or him? I don't understand.

—You do!

—Do I? Well, I don't know about that.

She looked at him closely. Was he making fun of her? His pale eyes slid away from her gaze. She changed course.

—George, please, I can't stand it here. Can you not see that? I'll go mad, I'll be like him, worse.

He looked at her directly then, for the first time, it seemed, since they had arrived, and she saw in his face the realisation dawning that she was indeed in pain. She smiled, and touched his hand. The door burst open and the old man came bounding in, waving his arms.

—They're swarming, they're swarming! Come on!

She held George's arm. He smirked at her in a travesty of appeasement, and wriggled out of her grasp. The old man disappeared from the doorway. George raced after him. When he reached the garden it was empty. The air throbbed with a deep, malevolent hum. He stumbled through the briars and the tangled grass, into the orchard, ducking under the branches. The old man lay on his back among the hives, eyes wide, the hose clutched in his hands, the water rising straight up and splashing back on his face. George knelt by his side, under the spray. The orchard quivered around him. Under the sun all was gloom and growth, green things, stalks, lichen, rot and wrack. He stared into thorns and sodden mould, drenched leaves, the purple hearts of roses. His flesh crawled. Then he saw the snails. They were everywhere in the wet, on the leaves, the trees, glued along slender stalks of grass, gleaming silver and black brutes straining out of their shells as though in ecstasy, their moist horns erect and weaving. It was a dance. The snails were dancing. A black cloud of bees rose from the hives and spun away into the sky, thrumming. The old man was dead.

George stood in the bedroom.

—I had better stay here for a day or two, he said. Clear things up. You know.

She nodded absently, wandering about the room, picking up things, a newspaper, clothes, a tube of lipstick. She seemed hardly to notice him, and avoided meeting his eyes. He stood in the drawing-room and watched her clatter away down the drive, stumbling in her high heels, and then he went down and pushed the piano against the door.

Glorious weather, days drenched with sun and the singing of larks, a lavender haze over the sweltering meadows, the silence trembling on the upper airs of evening, and then the nights, the glossy black and the pale radiance, Sirius ascending, a smokewhite breeze at dawn. He spent his time in the garden, tending the roses, the vegetables, the hives. Sometimes he took the hose and sprayed the parched plants, the trees, the earth, and then sat for hours studying the surging life around him, the spiders, the birds and flies, his beloved bees. A swarm of them settled in a corner of the drawing-room, under the ceiling. That was fine with him. Life everywhere.

AUTHOR'S NOTE

Eight of these nine stories were published, under the title *Long Lankin*, by Secker & Warburg, London, in 1970. Another story, "Persona," and a longer tale, or novella, called "The Possessed," I have decided not to republish. For the present edition, slight revisions to the 1970 text have been made, mainly in punctuation. The final story here, "De Rerum Natura," was first published in the *Transatlantic Review*.

November 1984